HE PUT HIS FOOT AGAINST A LOOSE BOULDER AND LEANED OVER. HELDON SAW HIM AND FIRED, AS GABE HAD EXPECTED.

As the bullets tore at the ledge, then at his feet, Gabe gave the rock a nudge. It went over and hit the ledge with a *whump*; the ledge hung for a moment, then fell, raining snow and rock on the men, wiping Heldon off the side, drowning his scream in its thunder, and sending the other men scurrying for the relative safety of the cliff face.

Hal had made it to the other side of the lower ledge, clear of the bulk of the cascading ice and earth.

But the mountain was just getting started. As the roar echoed around him, Gabe heard, then felt, the peak above begin to rumble. He looked up and saw powder rise from the deep snow overhead. Snowball-sized chunks began to break away, picking up more snow as they fell and kicking other pieces loose.

Suddenly, the entire mountainside began to slide …

CLIFFHANGER

A NOVEL BY JEFF ROVIN
BASED ON THE SCREENPLAY BY
MICHAEL FRANCE AND
SYLVESTER STALLONE
SCREEN STORY BY MICHAEL FRANCE
BASED ON A PREMISE BY JOHN LONG

A SIGNET BOOK

SIGNET

Published by the Penguin Group
Penguin Books Ltd, 27 Wrights Lane, London W8 5TZ, England
Penguin Books USA Inc., 375 Hudson Street, New York, New York 10014, USA
Penguin Books Australia Ltd, Ringwood, Victoria, Australia
Penguin Books Canada Ltd, 10 Alcorn Avenue, Toronto, Ontario,
Canada M4V 3B2
Penguin Books (NZ) Ltd, 182–190 Wairau Road, Auckland 10, New Zealand

Penguin Books Ltd, Registered Offices: Harmondsworth, Middlesex, England

First published in the USA by Jove Books, a division of Putnam Berkley Group Inc., 1993
First published in Great Britain 1993
13 5 7 9 10 8 6 4 2

Published by arrangement with the Putnam Berkley Group Inc.

Signet Film and TV Tie-in edition first published 1993

Printed in England by Clays Ltd, St Ives plc

PROLOGUE

Mountain-making, or orogeny, takes millions of years and comes about in many ways. Most typically, it occurs when an underwater trench fills with mineral and organic silt, sediment that is crushed and hardened over the millennia into sedimentary rock. This rock is subjected to even greater pressure as more rock piles on or the crustal plates shift or the trench floor itself starts to rise.

Sometimes the rock liquefies, pouring up through volcanoes. More often, the rock refuses to go soft and is squeezed up from the trench, buckling as it's pushed toward the sky, forming great, craggy walls dozens of miles wide and hundreds of miles long.

Pressure. It's constant, unyielding pressure that builds the greatest peaks.

Geologists classify mountain ranges in the same way that living things are measured: youth, maturity, and old age. To be as old as the hills is to be ancient indeed, reduced from cloud-piercing splendor to rolling, grass-covered senility, whittled away over a half-billion years by melting snow, windblown sand, and other erosive forces.

The Rocky Mountains are a young, tall, rough range.

Formed just sixty-five million years ago, they sprawl from New Mexico to Alaska and reach heights of up to twenty thousand feet.

Like any youth, the Rockies are unpredictable and fickle, with countless secrets. Though their beauty is seductive, they're a demanding suitor: once in their embrace, you need extraordinary stamina to perform, to endure.

The Rockies are also unforgiving. Let down your guard, look up when you should look down, take one step left instead of right, and you'll become insignificant particles of sediment in some future range.

Mountain-making, or orogeny, takes millions of years.

Death—or murder—takes an instant.

ONE

Its tail slightly raised, rotor tilted ahead, the Huey Ranger sliced through the mountain range, climbing at one hundred and fifty miles an hour. The helicopter's speed and angle suggested purpose, and the loud echo of its engines announced its coming—the cavalry given wing, a guardian angel of the lost or stranded or careless.

But it was the mountains that made the sound so large. Taillight spinning, sun glinting off its clear cockpit, the rescue ship itself was a bug, a firefly, as it followed the sheer face of the Tower, a rectangular peak just a few feet under a mile high.

Tenuous clouds circled the mountain's middle and thicker clouds hid its summit; Jessie Deighan angled off the chopper's sharp ascent as it neared the lower bank of clouds.

A voice and slightly labored breathing came clearly through her headset. "Do you see them yet?"

Jessie Deighan smiled and adjusted her microphone; damn thing always slid down after a sharp bank like the one she'd just made.

"Patience, my love, patience."

The sun gleamed off her sunglasses as she swung the Ranger around to the north side of the peak. Jessie's smile broadened as she listened to him panting. "Mountaineering's a young man's sport, Gabe."

Beside her, Frank Newell made a face behind his binoculars and pulled a stick of gum from the vest pocket of his Rocky Mountain Park jacket. He unwrapped it and folded it into his mouth, his eyes never leaving the peak. "Bring her closer, Jess. Up ahead is where they're supposed to be. And watch it."

"What?"

"You're in your thirties too, remember?"

Jessie edged the helicopter closer to the Tower. "You hear that, Gabe? My half-century-something-old spotter says we're *both* over the hill."

Gabe snorted. "Yeah, I heard. But not *this* hill. This one's still way over me."

Jessie's smile warmed. In the years she'd known Gabe Walker, he'd developed crow's feet, aches in his lower back, and a Whitney Houston taste in music. In just the two years they'd been living together, he no longer watched Nick at Night after they made love. He went to sleep.

But God bless his sense of humor. It was still as quick and strong as when they first met, back when they were students in Denver, geology majors who decided to chuck the ivory tower for the real things, the pillars of the earth. The flesh might be weak, but the spirit was still a blast.

She often wondered if ten or more years together would have done to their relationship what it had done to their bodies . . . What would have happened if she hadn't come here but had gone with him abroad, spending years accompanying expeditions up every important mountain from Kilimanjaro to K2, doing what he did best while, he said, he could still do it—

4

There was a bright light to the right, a flare. Hal's.

"Got 'em!" Frank said, snapping his fingers, forming them into a gun, and pointing toward the cliff, just under the burst of red.

Jessie was suddenly all business. "Gabe? I think we have them sighted."

"I heard."

"What's the word, Frank?"

The spotter refocused the powerful Celetronic. "The word is"—he leaned forward and squinted toward the jagged brown wall—"we *got* 'em. Over there! See 'em?"

Jessie looked to where he was pointing, toward a peak that was part of the Tower, lower and separated by a chasm over two hundred feet wide. She saw the ledge and the fading flare in the hand of one of the climbers.

"I see them," Jessie said.

As the chopper neared, she could make out two figures in their warm-weather climbing gear. Hal was sitting, his knee wrapped in an elastic bandage. He didn't seem to be in pain and began waving a flare gun as the chopper approached. Hal was a good ranger, but he had no business climbing on his day off. He'd been on two rescues the day before and should have been resting.

Sarah was sitting next to him. Her knees were pressed together, and she didn't look happy to be there. Hal certainly had no business bringing a first-timer up the Tower.

"Poor thing's probably scared to death," Jessie muttered. She lowered her gaze and said into the microphone, "Gabe? Gabe, where are you?"

"Just hangin' out."

Her eyes narrowed, crawled slowly down the mountain wall, over the small outcroppings, some dusted with early snow, over the splits and crevices that afforded even experienced climbers barely a fingerhold. She didn't see him.

"*Where* are you?"

"Here."

She grinned as she dropped her gaze to a fat ledge. "My God," she said softly, as she saw why Gabe was panting.

He looked like a spider, clinging to the underside of the ledge, which was a killer, leaving Gabe hanging upside down in his black outfit and brown boots. There was a taut rope under his backside, hooked to a piton on either side.

She whistled appreciatively.

Gabe chuckled into the headset. "Careful, Jess. You'll intimidate Frank."

Frank trained his glasses on the cliff. "It'll take a heap more than that, rock jock. So tell me: you resting or showing off?"

"Neither," said Gabe. "I'm waitin' for someone to tell me where the lovebirds are."

Frank said, "They're about two hundred feet from the top of the Tower, right where the next ledge comes out, Gabe. You know that spot?"

"He knows it well," Jessie said, trying to hold the chopper stationary in the rising thermals.

Gabe had already hammered pitons closer to the lip and was slinging a rope between them.

"We spent a month there one night . . ." Gabe said. Jessie watched as he held on to a pair of rocks overhead and slid on his back from the sling-rope he was on to the one he'd just rigged. He moved with the grace of a big cat, his attention on the climb, his muscles moving smoothly beneath his clothing. Despite the arduous climb, his strong arms showed no sign of weakness or strain. If there ever came a time when she couldn't stand the rest of him, she'd still love those arms.

When he reached the top, Gabe waved at the helicopter. Then he slipped an ice hammer from his belt and started tapping in pitons, building a makeshift ladder to cover the last hundred feet. Even that he did with intense concentration; the climber who got sloppy, who took the smallest detail for granted, ended up taking the shortest route back down the mountain. Worse, he endangered the lives of everyone in the party.

Gabe was experienced, which meant he didn't go faster than novices. He took the time to do the job right.

When he was finished, he put a foot in the loop to test it. When he was satisfied he began climbing, hooking himself on with his safety belt each time he stopped to pound in a new piton. "Years ago, when I was seventeen thousand feet up Elbrus, I realized that if I stopped to *think* about what I was doing—hanging by a thread somewhere near God's beard—I'd realize I was nuts and never do it again."

"So you stopped thinking."

"I stopped *worrying*. I'm like the mountain. You can't change what you are, and you sure can't hide what you are. So you might as well just *be* it."

Jessie shook her head. "It's amazing, Frank, how you can live with a guy and be so blinded by love that you don't realize what an *asshole* he is."

Frank snickered and covered the mike. "Gabe's pretty blinding."

"Yeah," Jessie said quietly, watching as he neared the ledge with the stranded climbers. He'd gone four thousand feet from the base of the Tower in just four hours since the search began. "And he's something else."

"What's that?"

7

She said loudly, into the mike, "Gabe, the wind's too strong—I can't land here. I'll put her down on the Tower and we'll string a line across."

He signaled an okay and Jessie throttled up the Huey, rising swiftly along the majestic face of the cliff.

TWO

"Room service," Gabe said as he pulled himself over the ledge. He pushed the short, dark hair from his forehead, then cupped his hands and blew into them, warming his ruddy, windblown cheeks. His dark eyes settled briefly on Sarah Collins. "Hi, Sarah."

"Hi, Gabe." She managed a little smile, but it was set in an ashen face.

Gabe's eyes fell to the figure at her feet.

The young man propped himself on an elbow. "Glad you could drop in."

"Hey, anything for a friend. How's the knee?"

"I think it's out." He patted it. "No big deal—except when you're four thousand feet up."

"Oh yeah, the knee," Gabe said, crawling over. He pulled off a glove and squeezed around the patella. "I remember when you twisted it getting out of the hot tub."

Hal rolled his eyes. Sarah's flashed.

"That's funny," she said. "You told me it was an old war wound from 'Nam."

Hal shot Gabe a look.

Gabe's mouth twisted. "Yeah." He slipped the radio from

9

his pocket. "Rescue One, have located injured climber. Please prepare a transport line."

Hal sat up, his long brown hair blowing in the wind. "Just wait. Payback's sweet," he said through his teeth.

"If I screw up, I'll deserve it." Gabe stood back from the ledge as the chopper moved in.

Jessie turned the Ranger ninety degrees, so the cabin's sliding door was facing the ledge. The door was cranked back and Frank appeared in the doorway. He locked a pulley into place overhead, then stood to the side. A cable began playing out, blown toward the ledge by the rotor wash.

Gabe stole a look at Sarah. She was sitting ramrod-straight against the cliff, eyes wide, arms stiff and pressing down on the ledge.

"How're ya feeling, Sarah?" Gabe shouted.

"Fine—I guess."

He gave her a thumbs-up, then turned back to the cable, which was just a few feet overhead. He jumped up to grab it, missed, and landed less than a foot from the edge.

"Gabe! *Jesus!*" Sarah gasped.

Gabe motioned the chopper toward him, shouted over his shoulder, "Sarah—this ledge is like the Great Plains compared to some of the places Hal an' I have been. Right, pal?"

"Sure, right!"

Gabe laughed as the cable was almost within reach. "Sarah," he said, "we could take off and leave this guy behind. . . ."

As Gabe jumped for the cable and snared it, Hal reached down and snatched his radio. "Rescue One, please be advised that Ranger Walker is making advances toward my girlfriend that are liable to get his ass kicked right into space. Over."

"Copy, Hal," Jessie said over the radio.

Hal grinned and held the radio up for Gabe to hear.

"Tell Gabe he only makes advances *to me* or else he'll be walking down four thousand feet, and sleeping outside."

Gabe walked forward with the cable and took a heavy piton from his hardware sling. "She's tough," he said.

"You know it," Jessie shot back.

The chopper settled gently on the opposite peak, which afforded a wider patch of rock than the one the climbers were on.

Frank climbed out, hunching slightly under the rotor, buffeted by the heavy winds. He watched as Gabe put the piton through the eye at the end of the cable and started whacking it into the cliff beside Sarah, forming a taut, level lifeline between the ledge and the Ranger.

The young woman crawled under the cable toward Hal. "Is it really four thousand feet?"

"Give or take a few." He smiled at her. "Look, I know you're nervous, but we've done this a hundred times." He put a gloved hand behind her head and pulled her toward him. He kissed her lips, then her forehead. "You're gonna be okay. Okay?"

"Okay."

"I mean it," he said.

She smiled bravely as Hal turned and clipped his climbing harness to the rescue line.

Gabe signaled the chopper and Frank waved back. Gabe turned to Hal.

"Remember: keep your arms and legs within the vehicle at all times—"

Hal grinned and clearly mouthed the words, *Fuck you.*

"No thanks," Gabe said sweetly.

Hal blew him a kiss, turned to the wire, then tripped and fell over the edge with a horrified shout. Sarah screamed

11

and lurched forward, reaching out to save him, but Gabe held her back.

Delighted with his little joke, Hal laughed gleefully from the safety of his harness, hung securely on the wire but still dangling four thousand feet in space, above the jagged rocks. He pulled himself rapidly across the line, hand over hand, completely oblivious to the vertiginous drop.

Realizing just how scared Sarah was, Gabe gave her a quick hug of encouragement before letting go of her.

On the other side of the line, Hal pulled himself the last few feet. Frank received him and unhooked the harness with a shake of his silver head. Hal limped to the open door of the Ranger and located a headset.

Gabe smiled at Sarah. "So, how did this clown ever talk you into climbing the Tower?" He was trying to get her mind off the impending journey across the wire.

Sarah glanced down. "He told me it was better than sex." She seemed embarrassed. But as she looked up and saw Hal, safe and secure, sitting in the open doorway of the chopper, she broke into a smile. "He made it!"

"Of course he did," Gabe said as he helped Sarah put on her backpack, a fuzzy stuffed dog strapped to the side.

Jessie's voice came over the radio. "Come on, guys, the winds are picking up."

"On my way," Gabe said through the headset, then turned to his still-frightened companion. "All right, Sarah, are you ready for the best ride in the park?"

She tried to smile back, but it wasn't quite there. "I'm sorry for all the trouble."

"Hey, it's nothing. We do it all the time."

"So, we're all still on for dinner tonight?"

She was trying to be casual. Gabe felt for her. "Of course."

She smiled and kissed his cheek.

Gabe turned and looked at Hal across the chasm. "Hey, did you see that?"

Hal laughed and waved back. Shooting Sarah a look of encouragement, he waved for Gabe to send her over.

Gabe held Sarah's arm gently as they moved closer to the edge of the cliff. He hooked her in and gave her hand a final squeeze, hoping to infuse her with the courage she badly needed.

"Ready?"

"Yeah."

"Just keep looking at me."

She nodded and slid off the ledge.

THREE

Sarah gasped as the wire bounced lightly under her weight. She hung there facing Gabe, her expression fearful but determined as she began the awkward hand-over-hand journey across the line.

Gabe held the wire steady from his end. Hal watched from the other side, his tension easing visibly as he watched her reach back to grasp the wire behind and above her, pulling herself several inches closer to safety. He looked across at Gabe and gave him a thumbs-up.

Sarah reached again over her head, grasped the wire awkwardly, moved another few inches.

Suddenly, a buckle on her rigging began to twist, the over-stressed metal softening, bending uncharacteristically out of shape. Sarah stopped moving and turned her head slightly.

Gabe pulled the wire tighter so it was absolutely still.

"Sarah, don't move!"

The buckle bent further until the metal finally cracked and the strap under Sarah's leg began to slip. She cried out over the sound of nylon whispering through metal.

"Oh, *God*! Hal—help!"

Hal yelled, "Sarah! Oh, shit!"

"I'm going to fall! Oh, God, help me!"

Hal shouted, "No, you're not! You're going to be okay. Can you reach the top line?"

A second strap, then a third strap began to slip. Sarah grasped on to the end of the strap as, within seconds, the entire harness unraveled around her.

"Help me! Please! Oh, God, help me!"

Gabe didn't dare move; the best thing he could do was keep the wire as steady as possible and hope the harness stabilized. As the nylon straps fed out through the network of hooks and fittings, the cracked buckle caught in the carabiner overhead and held. Sarah was left dangling from the end of a strap, five feet below the cable, held only by the frail buckle. Gabe knew it wouldn't hold for very long.

Hal screamed, "Hold on!" as he struggled to pull off his own harness. Frank helped, fumbling with the hooks. "I'm going to send my harness over—grab it!"

"No! I can't!"

"You *have* to, baby!"

Sarah's harness continued to come apart, each inaudible *pop* dropping her a little lower.

"Gabe—" Jessie was on the radio, her voice hard.

"Here."

"You've got to get her."

Gabe released the wire and moved back from the ledge.

"Gabe—" Jessie repeated.

"Yeah. I'm coming out."

Hal yelled into his headset. "No! The line's not rigged to hold two people! I'm sending out my harness!"

Gabe screamed back, "The clip's not going to hold!"

Jessie came over the headset again. "Gabe! You've got to go after her!"

Sarah was swinging like a pendulum on the wire—helpless, her exhausted hands weakening.

"I'm slipping," she cried faintly. "Please, please . . ."

Hal continued to struggle frantically with his harness. "No! Hold on, baby!"

Gabe called out. "*Forget* the harness. There's no time! I'm going for her."

Hal looked like he wanted to argue. Instead, he gave up removing his harness and, digging himself in, grabbed the cable to steady it.

Hurrying over to the line, Gabe gently pulled himself up and, lifting his legs, crossed his ankles around it. He clipped himself on with a three-foot safety line and quickly started pulling himself out as smoothly as possible.

Hal was in anguish. "Don't lose her, Gabe! I've got the line! Don't sway it—"

He fell silent as the combination of the winds and the bobbing of the line from Gabe's weight made her lose her grip even faster.

Gabe pulled himself along, hurrying but trying not to shake the cable. He was as intense as before, aware of everything that was happening, of the importance of every action, of every second. He looked across at Hal to reassure him.

"Be easy on the line, Gabe!"

Sarah started to look down into the abyss.

"No!" Gabe shouted. "Keep looking at me—Sarah! Don't look down, look at me!"

Her eyes slid up, wide and terrified.

"That's it . . . keep your eyes on me. You can do it. You're stronger than you think!"

He was only ten feet away.

Jessie's voice was in his ear again. "Gabe, hurry—you can do it. A little more and you've got her."

Gabe inched forward, head tilted back so he could see

Sarah. The wind turned her around completely, and when she was facing him again her mouth was wide with fear, her head and arms trembling.

All you need to do is grab a part of her, Gabe told himself.

Eight feet away. His eyes held hers, and as he watched the buckle started to open. Sarah dropped a few more inches; the jerk caused the small, stuffed dog to tumble from her backpack. Her eyes followed it as it fell.

"No!" Gabe screamed. "Keep looking at me!"

Sarah was transfixed by the dog as it plunged through the void.

"*Sarah*! Don't look down—look at me!"

Slowly, almost painfully, she brought her head up.

"That's it," Gabe said, inching ahead. "Keep your eyes on me. You can do it."

But Sarah's grip loosened. As she began to slip lower, she made a desperate grab for the line above.

"Shit," Gabe cried out. "She's losing it."

"She's not losing it!" Hal screamed. "Sarah! He'll have you in a second. Hold on, goddammit! You can do it. If you fall, I'll fucking kill you!"

Gabe was less than three feet away. "I'm here," he said, craning his head around so he was face-to-face. "Sarah, I'm here."

He was two feet away. He twisted an arm so that it was under him. His hand was just a foot from hers.

"Reach up!" Hal yelled. "Grab him!"

Sarah rolled her eyes up, pressed her lips together, and tried to pull herself up.

"That's it," Gabe said. He hooked one leg over the cable and let the other dangle so he was on his side, his hand just inches away. "One big heft is all you—"

"*Gabe!*"

He watched in horror as the buckle burst over her head, the rope played out through the hook, and what was left of the harness dropped.

There wasn't even time to swear. Gabe threw himself off the cable, grabbed for her, and caught her outstretched arm. The harness and rope fell away like a fluttering bird, and his own safety line snapped taut, springing him and Sarah up and down. Within moments, the winds started pushing them back and forth.

"Fucking goddamn!" Hal cried in the cabin. "Don't lose her, Gabe. Don't you drop her!"

Gabe looked down at Sarah. With her as dead weight, there was no way he could reach the cable. But if he could get her up . . .

"Sarah," he said, "I'm gonna reach down for you with my other hand. I need you to take it."

She brought her arm around, but they couldn't connect. She began to twist in the wind, making it difficult for Gabe to hold her.

"Help me!" she sobbed. "I don't want to die!"

"You're not gonna die. Try again. Reach up and grab me."

Hal yelled, "Come on! You can do it. *Now!* Do it *now!*"

She tried again, but the force of her swing caused her other arm to slip down. Gabe squeezed hard on her wrist, lost it, hooked his fingertips under her climbing glove.

"*Make a fist!*" he shouted. "It'll hold the glove on!"

She did. It held. She gasped as the fabric cut into her wrist.

Hal was growling into the radio. "Don't lose her, Gabe! Don't lose her!"

Gabe's arm ached, and despite the bitter cold, his face was red, perspiration dripping down his neck. He looked down at her, imploring.

"Another try, Sarah. One big swing and I've got you."

He stretched his hand out. She looked up at his face.

"Come on, honey!" Hal was shouting. "I love you, baby. You can do it! Reach up. *Reach up!*"

Sarah just hung there. Gabe knew she was spent, and painfully he tried to pull her up while he arced his own arm toward her.

She came up, unable to help him, inches at a time, Gabe stretching to grab her coat, her backpack, anything—

And then her fist opened.

Gabe watched helplessly as she slid from the glove. She didn't spread her arms and legs as a skydiver does; she just fell, her eyes locked on his, her scream all around as she plummeted toward the distant earth.

"*No!*" Hal screamed. "*NO!!*"

Gabe twisted on his safety line, clutching Sarah's glove, shaking with exhaustion and anger, unable to watch and looking up, locking eyes with Hal.

The scream grew faint, and in moments it was just a memory that would be with him always, like the tortured face of his friend and the awful eternity of the four-thousand-foot fall.

Nineteen seconds to bottom. *She wasn't even dead yet.*

"Gabe—"

It was Jessie's voice, softer than before.

"You did more than anyone could have expected."

But it wasn't enough.

"Gabe, come back in."

Tears came to Gabe's eyes and he squeezed them shut.

Dead. She was dead and so was he. He'd died before she had, only something inside wouldn't let him join her.

He reached up. Lighter by one human being, he was able now to reach the cable, and he began the slow and painful trip back. . . .

FOUR

The United States Mint was established in Philadelphia in 1792. Copper penny and half-penny pieces were minted for general circulation the following year, silver coins were introduced the year after that, and gold coins were minted in 1795.

Today, coins and paper have very little value in and of themselves; a dime does not contain ten cents' worth of metal, nor a ten dollar bill ten dollars' of paper. The value of money is that people accept it in exchange for products or services.

In 1969, the United States Mint stopped issuing general circulation currency in denominations over one hundred dollars. Removing one thousand, five thousand, and ten thousand dollar bills from circulation made the work of the counterfeiter a little less lucrative. And thousand dollar bills had little practical use anyway: people weren't flashing them in Times Square to buy their theater tickets.

Denominations of one thousand to one hundred thousand dollars were still being printed, but only for use in transactions between the Federal Reserve System and the Treasury Department, and for exchanges in international banking.

The fact that relatively few people dealt in these denominations made them extremely valuable. Because they were moved quickly and only between banking institutions, it was virtually impossible for them to be stolen. Because only authorized personnel had access to them, it was virtually impossible for counterfeiters to obtain them. When presented to the proper institution, they were not questioned.

They're lighter than gold. They're rarer than gold.

They're better than gold.

FIVE

As the stack of thousand dollar bills moved along the belt, a thin mechanical hand shot from the left, squeezed and lifted the bills, and held them as a robot hand on the right pressed a paper band around them. That hand swung the stack to a growing pile in a deep metal box on the side as the first arm extended to meet the next stack.

The entire process took just over a second.

Richard Travers turned the electronic card key over and over in his hand, watching without emotion as the box filled with stacks one hundred bills deep. Each box held three hundred and four stacks, thirty-four million dollars in all; two other boxes had already been filled.

One hundred million dollars plus. He thought about the long, green paycheck in his wallet and felt humbled. It was like having a dick a micron long.

When the third box was filled, the treasury agent inserted the key in a slot above the mechanical hands. The machine stopped cold. The big room at the Treasury Department's southwest regional printer and distributing center was silent.

The big man put the silver card in his wallet and took out another, which he slipped into each of the boxes in turn. As

22

he did, he heard a faint *click-click,* and a red light flashed above each slot.

He placed the card in his wallet and looked down at the trio of boxes.

One hundred million dollars. He was ready to do his thirty-million-dollar part.

The door opened behind him and a uniformed man entered.

"We'll be fueled and ready in ten minutes, Mr. Travers."

"Very good."

The pilot left, and Travers took one last glance at the boxes.

Winning the lottery. Being a king. Getting laid every night. It was all there in those three big boxes.

Footfalls on the tile floor snapped him from his musings. He turned as Head Comptroller Wright entered the room, right behind somebody he didn't know but who reeked of *straight.*

Wright nodded as he walked over. "Rich—"

"Good morning, Walt."

"—I'd like to have a word with you. This is Agent Matheson, F.B.I."

No shit, Travers thought. "Richard Travers," he said, extending his hand.

"Matheson has been transferred from the Denver office to Frisco," Wright said. "As a professional courtesy between offices, I was asked if he could hitch a ride."

"We've got a full crew—"

"Anyone you can leave behind?"

Travers looked from the lantern-jawed agent to the big, black comptroller.

"Not really, but— Hell, we can squeeze in one more, Wright."

"Appreciate it."

"You're the boss." He looked at his watch then gestured toward the door. "Let's head out to the tarmac. Matheson, have you been totally briefed?"

"I don't know about totally—"

Travers laughed and patted him on the shoulder as they walked down a brightly lit corridor.

"Who the hell ever is? Let me bring you up to speed. This is the most protected shipment we've got—and the most useless."

"How so?"

"These bills here aren't even *in* circulation; the one thousand dollar bills we're transporting today are only used for international banking exchange."

"I see. So your average, garden-variety thief wouldn't even be interested."

Travers nodded.

"Do you always transport through the air?"

"Mostly," Wright answered. "Armored cars can be hijacked. Trains can be derailed. But nobody can get to us in flight."

Travers frowned. "I haven't lost a bill in eighteen years. Don't jinx me, Walt."

Wright laughed. "I think Treasury personnel are *the* most superstitious people in the federal government."

"We should be. There's always someone out there who wants what we've got."

The men turned the corner, signed out with the security guard, and entered an elevator.

Two minutes later, they were on the tarmac and headed toward the waiting DC-9.

SIX

As the battered Land Rover sailed up the mountain road, Gabe noticed that the clouds were rolling in.

An early winter storm was in the offing, but Gabe didn't mind. To the contrary. It had been eight months since he'd seen the rugged peaks of the Rockies, tasted the mountains, felt the cold bite of the wind and snow.

Eight months since they'd buried Sarah.

There was never a day when he didn't think of her, never a night that he didn't lie in bed, reliving her fall, going back to the moment when he lost her, only this time holding on—

Gabe tried to shake the thought as he passed the gas station on the outskirts of town, the road narrowing immediately as it crossed into the National Forest. He was oblivious to the two young rock jocks finishing up at the gas pumps.

Brett, a sun-bleached blond, squinted through his glacier glasses as the Land Rover sped by.

"Evan, that was Gabe!" The young man began gesturing wildly. "Hey, man! *Gabe!*"

The two leapt into their well-worn Jeep and swung from the station, trailing rock and roll music and burning rubber.

25

Evan honked the horn, though it was the loud music that pulled Gabe's eyes to the rearview mirror. He slowed a bit as he recognized the familiar faces, let them pull alongside.

Evan leaned across his buddy and called out, "How you doin', Gabe?"

"Hey, Brett. Hey, Evan."

Gabe knew that he didn't sound like himself. He never did when he tried to match the youthful energy of kids—only now, against the enthusiasm of their welcome, he felt the dead spot inside him even more acutely.

Evan grinned, his white teeth contrasting with the deep, ever-present tan of his skin. "Where ya been, man?"

Gabe managed a casual smile. "Working. In Denver."

"Work!" Brett shuddered. "Don't say that word, man."

"Man," Evan chimed in, "I hate work even when somebody else is doing it!"

"Hey, Gabe," Brett said, "we're flyin' off the Tower today. C'mon with us."

"Yeah, man. It's perfect weather for a killer jump."

"No, thanks."

"Come on, Gabe," Brett said. "Don't tell me that job in Denver made you scared of heights."

Gabe's reaction was slight, a small stiffening of the neck, a sadness about the eyes. He wondered if the boys saw it.

He shook his head, trying to shake the sorrow, at least outwardly.

"There's a storm up there," Gabe said. "You guys watch out for it."

Brett beamed. "We like it extreme."

"Yeah," said Evan. "Well, later, Gabe."

The two waved as Gabe slipped ahead. He glanced in the rearview mirror and saw them watching him as they made a U-turn.

Even they noticed.

He had to get out of here. Do what he came to do and leave. Not because he felt he could escape what had happened, but because he didn't want to be where everyone knew, where people smiled as he approached, then pitied him as he passed.

He pushed the Land Rover ahead, the Rockies blue-grey and looming, the skies above them dark and getting more so by the minute. . . .

SEVEN

The house was small, rustic, set on six acres and made of local lumber and stone. A spacious corral was built just north of the house, where it got the sun from ten in the morning on, once it cleared the mountains. There was a small red barn just west of the corral.

Jessie was grooming her new horse, a bay. The wind was blowing gently, scattering hay around the corral; the cold knifed through her, invigorating her.

The horse whinnied and stepped back.

Jessie frowned. "Come here, you. The cold's good for—"

"How ya' doin', Jess?"

Jessie gasped and turned quickly. Her face froze with shock, but only for a moment. She turned to continue grooming the horse. She whispered to quiet the uneasy animal.

Gabe looked past her. "Got a new horse?"

"Yes."

"What's its name?"

"Twiglet. Where've *you* been?"

He moved a shoulder. "Working—odd jobs. Trying to figure out where to start."

"Maybe I can help. Let's see. . . . If one night I got up and packed all my things and drove away without leaving so much as a note, and stayed away for months, I think what I'd want to do is explain myself, apologize, then go." She glared at him. "What do *you* think?"

"I think I deserved that."

"Glad you agree. There's more—"

"Jess, I know that what I did wasn't right. But after the funeral, I just had to leave."

"Had to leave? Why?"

"A lot of things fell apart on that ledge."

"I know."

"I don't think you know how much."

Jessie took a step forward. "Oh, yes, I do. I saw it when you tried to talk to Hal. I saw it every time I looked at you looking out the window or staring at the ceiling or sitting on the fence looking out at the mountains. Oh, Gabe—I *do* know. And I also know something else. You did your best to save her. Why can't *you* believe that?"

"Did I? I don't know. Maybe I shouldn't have gone out on that line, like Hal said. Maybe I panicked . . . I don't know."

"But I *do*. You were the only one who didn't panic. You were the guy hanging ass-down on a sagging cable three-quarters of a mile up. You were the guy who jumped after her and *caught* her. You did everything that could be done. So do us all a favor—don't hoard all the guilt. And what about Hal?"

"What about him?"

"Christ, Gabe! What was *he* doing up on the Tower with a girl who could barely climb?"

"He did fine until he got hurt. I can't blame anything on Hal. It was me. I play it back in my mind every day."

29

"Then turn it off, Gabe, because it doesn't get any better."

He looked at her. "Just turn it off? I don't think you understand."

"I don't understand? I think maybe I'm the only one who *does* understand. Gabe, who did you live with for two years? Who stood by you, who did you make promises to, who spent too many nights looking up at these mountains and wondering if you were ever going to make it down in one piece . . . or ever at all? Believe me, there've been times I didn't know what I wanted to do more, love you or be able to hate you. But the one thing I did know and still do know is that I understand you. And Gabe—this guilt is a mountain you just can't climb."

Gabe looked into her eyes and touched her hair. Jessie moved toward him and put her head on his chest.

"Gabe—did you come back to stay?"

He said nothing. She took a step back.

"You didn't."

"I can't, Jess. Not here. What I came back for is you. If you want . . . I mean, I'd like you to come with me."

"Where?"

"Somewhere. I don't know. Anywhere but here."

Jessie turned, grabbed a bucket and walked away. Thunder rumbled in the distance.

Gabe followed as she headed toward the house.

"You're a bastard," she sobbed. "You come back after being gone almost a year, from God knows where—"

"Denver. And there wasn't a day went by that I didn't want to call."

"Then why didn't you?" She spun. "*That* was cowardice, Gabe, not what you did up there on the Tower."

"I'm sorry. I needed to be alone."

"And what about what *I* needed?"

"You didn't need a basket case."

"I needed *you*!"

Jessie turned away.

Gabe looked at the ground. "Do you still need me?"

"Figure it out."

He took a deep breath. "Will you come with me then, Jess?"

She faced him and said without hesitation, "No. This was our home . . . and now it's *my* home. I can't leave. You can stay with me, and believe me, I want you to. I've been lonely and I've been hurting, and as much as I hate to admit it, I want you. But to just take off for the wrong reasons, I can't do it. And neither should you."

"Yeah, well—like I said, I can't turn it off."

"And I can't leave."

There was a long silence. Gabe's look was imploring, and Jessie started to come forward; she stopped.

She wanted to hold him, hug him tightly, get closer than he'd let her during those long, awful months after the accident. But it would be wrong. His guilt would consume them both and destroy them.

Gabe blinked hard, then zipped his windbreaker and looked toward the house. "I understand," he said quietly.

"I'm sorry."

"No—it's okay. If it's all right with you, I'm gonna pick up the rest of my gear."

"You know where everything is. I didn't move any of it." She took a quick look at her watch. "I'm . . . I'm late for my shift."

He nodded. "Everybody okay?"

"Yeah. Frank's Frank, Hal is . . . Hal."

Gabe came toward her. "Tell them . . . I miss them. Okay?"

Jessie nodded once and hurried to her Jeep.

31

EIGHT

The Treasury jet roared into the sky, soaring toward the mountains and the great, rolling thunderclouds backlit by the early morning sun.

The DC-9 hopped a little as it flew over the foothills, caught by the constantly shifting currents. Matheson gripped the handrest tightly as the plane was jostled.

"Nervous?"

Matheson looked over at Treasury Agent LoDolce, who was scrunched in the bank of seats across the aisle; a second agent, Kidd, dozed in the seat beside his partner. There was gear in the seat beside Matheson; Travers was sitting in front of him.

"I'm ex-Navy, below-the-deck radar," Matheson said. "Never did like the air."

"Me neither," said LoDolce. "So what happens? I end up waltzin' through the clouds, baby-sitting T-bills. Travers says you're being transferred."

Matheson looked over to LoDolce. "Yeah," he said. "Moving up in the world."

"Movin' up," said the agent wistfully, drumming on his knee. "I'm waitin' to move down. Desk job somewhere.

32

Gotta have ten years in the field before you get that, though. Like Mr. Travers, here."

Travers appeared not to have heard. He was looking out the window.

Matheson turned and looked out his window as well. He squinted into the sun, which had broken through a bank of clouds.

Something had risen in front of the sun and stayed there. Something long and narrow. Another aircraft.

NINE

Sheets of rain slashed down from the storm clouds, drumming hard on the roof of the ranger station. The two-room cabin was perched high in the foothills. A satellite dish was sunk in concrete behind it; some eighty yards to the south, the Huey Ranger sat on a flat rocky shelf, secured by thick cables. A pair of muddy 4×4's were parked beside the dirt road that wound up through the foothills to the isolated spot.

Inside the cabin, Hal Tucker was sitting in a swivel chair, frowning as snow crept across the small TV screen on the corner of the desk.

"We need a bigger dish," he complained. "This thing's wobblin' like a happy dog's tail."

Frank put a dab of yellow on the canvas he was painting, then stepped back.

"What the heck are you complaining about? Denver ain't had a basketball team worth watching since the Cretaceous, and that picture's better'n the shit we used to get with the antenna."

"Yeah," Hal said, "but the guy who sold it to me said the wind wouldn't affect it."

"He said *shouldn't*. I was there, remember? And you didn't tell him you were putting it up in the middle of a goddamn mountain range." Frank threw a streak of black across the painting. "Besides, nobody stopped you from getting cable here."

"Right. Only need what—about sixty miles?"

The door flew open and Jessie hurried in. She wiped her face in her sleeve, shook her hands, and walked to the coffeepot.

"Hi, Jess," Frank said.

"Hi."

Hal looked over. "Don't you own a raincoat?"

"I was late—didn't get to listen to the weather."

"Wouldn't've mattered," he snickered. "They predicted sun. How was your day off?"

Jessie took her Jack Russell terrier mug off the pegboard over the sink and poured coffee.

"Jess?"

"Huh?"

"How was your day off?"

"It was okay."

"How is he?"

She fired him a look.

Hal's brow wrinkled. "Jess, what's wrong?"

"How do you know about him?"

"I know about him because you took the day off to ride him, remember? Twiglet. The new horse."

Jessie smiled. "Oh yeah. Sorry, Hal, my mind was somewhere else. Twig's fine. He's cute."

Frank dabbed on more yellow, then stepped back. "Oh yes, that's it right here. I believe ol' Frank nailed it with that stroke. Hal, c'mere."

Hal rolled over on the chair.

"No, you gotta stand. Get the full impact."

35

Hal shook his head and rose slowly. "Come on over, Jessie. You're just in time for another masterpiece."

Hands on his hips, Hal stood beside Frank.

"So? What do you see?"

"Dunno."

"What usually eats a banana?"

Hal looked from the canvas to Frank. "A monkey?"

"So . . . what are you, blind, son?"

Hal squinted toward the canvas. "Uh—no. Yeah, I see it. Sure."

Frank scowled. "Don't patronize me." He pointed with the back of the brush. "This is a banana eating a monkey, nature in reverse."

Hal nodded slowly. "I see. Well, I'll say this. At least there's no static, Frank. Real clear picture."

The ranger shook his head. "You're pathetic."

Jessie smiled as she walked to the window, staring out as she sipped her coffee. Hal turned his attention back to the TV.

And the rain continued to beat straight down, mixed with hail as a cold front moved in from the north. . . .

TEN

Through the window of the Treasury jet, Matheson continued to watch the other aircraft. The Jet Star was getting closer, and not by chance. Its speed and movement were too precise.

He stood up. "We're being tracked!"

LoDolce turned to his boss. "Travers? We're not supposed to have anyone riding shotgun this flight."

"Stay put," Travers said calmly but in a sharp tone. "Don't anyone jump to conclusions."

Matheson looked out again at the Jet Star, which was getting closer.

Travers rose and said, "I'll see if I can raise them on the radio."

His expression grave, the agent walked quickly through the cabin, knocked on the cockpit door, and entered. He shut the door behind him and looked at the instrument panel.

The pilot stole a glance back. "He's coming in too slow."

"No, we're going too fast, and we're too high up. Give me one hundred eighty knots and drop to fifteen thousand feet."

"One eight-zero, one-five thousand. Roger."

The copilot said nothing, but watched with confusion as the pilot throttled back and eased the U-shaped control forward. The DC-9 began to nose down.

Travers left the cockpit and joined the others.

Matheson was still standing, bent over the window. The other two agents were on their feet, huddled beside him. They were unaware of Travers's return.

"Christ," the G-man said, "we're losing altitude and slowing down!"

"Maybe Travers is trying to shake him."

"Standard op for evasion is bank, dive, speed up. This is just the opposite." Matheson looked back at the men. "If you have automatic weapons, get them!"

The two turned toward their seats. Travers was behind them, blocking them.

"What are you doing?"

"Travers, Matheson thinks—"

"Matheson doesn't have jurisdiction on this jet. I do."

Matheson looked from the window to Travers. "I wasn't questioning your authority, Travers. But we *are* being chased." He opened his briefcase and withdrew an automatic weapon.

Travers's gaze bore into the young agent. "Sit down. I'll make the determination whether or not we're being pursued and, if so, how to deal with it."

Matheson pointed the gun at him.

"What the hell are you doing?" Travers demanded.

"Now *I* have jurisdiction, *sir*." He glanced at the other agents. "I said get your weapons."

"LoDolce and Kidd are highly trained agents, Mr. Matheson," Travers said. "You're overreacting. There's no reason for this."

Travers put his hands out and walked forward, slowly backing Matheson toward the aisle. He made calming gestures as the other agents watched, ready to move, their eyes on the gun.

"Matheson, calm down and give the gun to me. You're out of control, son."

"What the hell are you waiting for?" Matheson shouted at the other agents. "Don't you see what he's doing? He's hijacking the shipment!"

LoDolce edged toward the aisle and joined Kidd as he stepped behind Matheson. The G-man stood a little taller, as though emboldened by their gesture.

But they weren't joining his ranks. The agents drew their weapons and held them on Matheson; Travers pulled out his own gun and aimed it at the G-man's head.

Matheson froze.

His gaze steady, Travers shifted the gun barrel to the left. He blasted LoDolce through the heart.

"Jesus!" Matheson screamed.

Kidd was stunned, but before he could react his boss turned again slightly and put a bullet between his eyes.

Then the gun swung back to Matheson. The G-man made a move toward Travers, but the agent fired again and Matheson flew backward, arms flailing, head jerking, his white shirt peppered with red. He landed in a heap in the aisle.

Travers took a moment to survey his handiwork. Behind him, the cockpit door clicked open and the copilot stepped out.

"God in heaven! What—"

He never found out. The pilot pulled a gun and the copilot flew forward, a puff of smoke rising behind him, a spray of blood painting the window red, as the pilot put a bullet in his brain.

Travers nodded once and the pilot returned to his seat. The agent immediately moved the bodies from the aisle, so they wouldn't be lost when he went to the second phase, then he opened the bag that had been belted to the seat beside Matheson. He tugged it open, withdrew a headset, and sat by the window.

The plane, a sleek Jet Star, was much nearer now, slightly behind the aircraft. Travers adjusted the mouthpiece.

"We're secure here. Move into position."

He watched as the door of the Jet Star slid open, then he rose and reached back into the bag.

ELEVEN

Travers quickly pulled on a windsuit and harness. He opened the security cage where the cables were stored, and began the slow process of dragging the heavy steel line to the rear of the plane. He was breathing heavily as he strapped on an oxygen mask and released the bolts in the tail cone.

The rush of air from the cabin was fierce as Travers opened the bulkhead door of the tail section. The vacuum it created sucked papers, pens, and even Matheson's briefcase from the jet.

Struggling against the rush of air, Travers moved to the right side of the cabin and pulled aside a tarp, revealing a big winch. Taking the cases of money one at a time, he connected each to a pulley and stacked them one on top of the other in the open doorway.

The Jet Star was behind and below them now. Travers futilely used one hand to shield himself from the 230-mile-an-hour wind, using the other to steady himself. Despite the tempest, he had no trouble making out the tall figure in the Jet Star doorway—the dark shape of Qualen.

Like Travers, Qualen was dressed in a cold-weather

jumpsuit, tied to a safety line, and wearing a headphone. Behind him, Travers saw the hulking, similarly attired forms of Ryan and Kynette.

Qualen's no-nonsense voice came over the earphones: "Ready."

Travers didn't answer; he went right to the winch. He knew that Qualen hated extraneous words or actions, hated anything that wasted his time.

Travers began to play the wire out, a thick strand of steel pushed up and out by the wind, arching up gracefully thanks to a lead weight at the end, with a hook the size of a coffee mug.

The line was on a trajectory that would carry it to the open door of the Jet Star.

"You're doing fine," Travers said into the microphone. "Come up a little more . . . more. . . . Keep proceeding. . . ."

The cable eased closer, the Jet Star eased upward, and the gap between the planes was just one hundred and fifty feet. Kynette reached out as the lead hook neared, snagged it with a shepherd's crook pole, and clipped it to a fulcrum welded to the floor of the Jet Star.

"Locked on," Qualen said into the mouthpiece. "Now the cases."

Travers picked up the cable he'd tossed aside, fastened one end to the winch line, ran the cable through the handles of each box, and clipped the other end to the line of the pulley system.

"Done!"

"Good," Qualen said. "Get the case. Kristel, move into transfer position."

Travers heard Qualen's pilot, Kristel, answer, "Check. Moving into transfer position."

She sounded tougher to Travers by half than his own pilot—than some of the pilots he'd known back in Southeast

Asia. But then, Qualen's pilot would be.

The Jet Star began to move forward, toward a position just under the DC-9. As it did so, Travers made his way back down the aisle. Entering the cockpit, he faced right and twisted the latch of the small compartment in which the pilots stored their personal effects.

"Travers!" the pilot shouted over his shoulder.

"Yeah."

"Take a look here. We're right on the edge of the storm! This isn't going to work!"

Travers threw the copilot's wallet and crossword puzzle book aside. "Don't lose your nerve! The storm'll help."

"What do you mean?"

Travers bent over a suitcase and opened it. Inside was an LED display, a switch, and several pounds of explosives—everything clean and compact, not like in 'Nam where he used to rig fertilizer bombs with gun cotton primers.

"This bomb is designed to leave nothing of itself behind. The investigators'll blame it on the storm. The plane got caught, lost its tail, and went down. The wreckage and body parts will make it look like six men were killed tragically in the line of duty."

Travers pressed the switch and the LED display started counting down.

"The bomb goes off in five minutes."

The pilot nodded.

Travers patted him on the shoulder. "Stick to the plan and you'll be rich."

Qualen's voice was in the headset.

"Travers! Hurry it up!"

"On my way," he said.

The agent hurried to the back of the plane. The plane was being rocked by the winds inside and out, and the bodies had shifted somewhat, sprawled again in the aisles.

Travers stepped over them; there was no time to push them back.

"Dip the plane," Travers said into the microphone. "I'm coming over."

Travers stood in the hole at the back of the plane and looked down. The Jet Star dropped directly beneath him, the winch line bowed slightly from the force of the wind.

He didn't stop to think about what would happen if the harness tore or the cable came loose or the Jet Star dropped a little or the DC-9 rose. He just thought *money*. Enough of it to live on, luxuriously, forever. *Money*, he told himself as he set the box down, hooked the harness to the cable, and grabbed the pulley. *Money*, he thought as he looked back.

The pilot was standing over the instrument panel. He threw a switch, putting the plane on auto, then moved down the aisle of the rocking cabin. It would take him fifteen seconds to loosen each bracket. Hook himself on. Get the boxes out. Maybe less, if he was scared enough.

Travers saluted him as he neared. The pilot saluted back. *Money*, Travers thought as he stepped out.

The cold punched right through the suit as he cleared the underside of the plane, stinging every inch of him as he rode down. The wind held his body horizontal as he fell, as if he were floating on rough seas. He could feel each rough eddy and wave as it punched him; he was amazed at how solid the air felt.

It was over in just ten seconds. Hands grabbed for him as he reached the door of the Jet Star. Kynette pulled him in; before Travers had his footing, Qualen had grabbed the front of his windsuit.

"Why didn't you send the money over?"

Travers unhooked himself, stepped back. "Somehow, I didn't think you'd wait for me if I sent it first."

44

Qualen's mouth, which had been twisted with rage, formed a smile. He patted Travers on the face. "Touché, Travers. You *do* surprise me now and then."

The agent didn't know which was worse: Qualen's anger, or how quickly it dissolved. The man was as unstable as the weather.

Qualen looked at his watch. "We're running out of time. I *assume* your pilot is coming—with the cases?"

"As we speak," he said.

Qualen leaned out; so did Travers. They saw the money boxes stacked in the opening, the pilot behind them.

Kristel shouted at them from the open cockpit door. A handsome woman in her early thirties.

"I can't hold this course much longer!" she yelled. "If you're gonna do something, do it now!"

Kynette sidled over to Travers. "What's keeping him?"

Travers adjusted his microphone. "Let's move your ass in there."

The pilot signaled from the back of the plane. He bent over the top box.

Travers looked at his own watch. A minute left. There was still plenty of time.

TWELVE

The pilot was sweating, perspiration evaporating behind his mask, fogging the lens. He squinted through the condensation as he made a quick, final check of the cases.

Everything was secure, the cases *and* his future. He was starting to feel very good about things as he reached down for the lever to release the cases. Once they were gone, he'd hook himself on and slide over, as Travers had done.

A raw shout turned him around.

"You . . . fuck—!"

Through the misty mask, the pilot made out the white and red form of Matheson, on his knees, leaning on an armrest. A gun was in his hand.

"No—!" the pilot screamed.

Matheson squeezed off a burst. The bullets tore into the pilot's thighs and threw him backward, blood spitting from his wounds. A second burst from the gun cut into his abdomen and punched him back through the opening. His foot tripped the release lever as he fell.

Blinded with sweat, burning with the pain of his wounds,

the pilot was oblivious to what was happening, even when his safety line went slack and he fell end over end through the charcoal clouds.

The cases started to move down the line. . . .

THIRTEEN

"What the hell!" Travers screamed as the pilot fell. He looked at his watch.

Half a minute.

Travers turned and shouted toward the cockpit. "Get underneath the jet! The cases will slide over!"

Kristel checked the vertical speed indicator. She adjusted the rudder trim and moved the control yoke; the Jet Star dipped sharply.

Travers and Qualen's other aide, Ray, leaned out.

"Shit!" Travers yelled as he saw Matheson in the opening and ducked back into the Jet Star. Ray didn't, and the burst of gunfire spun him against Qualen. His eyes were still open, his head lolling to one side.

Qualen shrugged him off. Kynette grabbed him.

"He's shot up bad. What do you want to do with him?"

"Get him to a hospital. Fast."

Kynette nodded. And shoved Ray out the door.

He hit the cable and bounced off. Qualen stole a quick look out. So did Travers. Matheson fired again, hitting windows and the fuselage.

Travers stepped back but continued to watch the jet. His

heart leaped as it lowered and the cases began to slide down.

"Yes!"

They rode the cable down. Oblivious to Matheson, Travers leaned out.

Come to papa!

They were halfway down . . . more.

Matheson fired another burst, stitching holes in the side of the Jet Star. Unfazed, Kristel held her course.

Travers looked at his watch. In just a few more seconds, the cases would be in their hands—

Suddenly, the back of the DC-9 disappeared, replaced by a black-and-orange fireball. The roar caused Travers to shriek and cover his ears. Windows blew out of the jet, pelting the Jet Star with shards of glass, and the ball expanded, ribbons of flame slicing through it. The DC-9 fuselage nosed down, the wings holding it steady for just a second, and then it started to turn onto its back.

Lightning flashed below as the red-glowing shell of the plane was swallowed in the thunderclouds. Pieces of scorched wallpaper and fabric from the seats, bags, and clothing swirled and spun in the plane's wake like black snow. Within moments, the Jet Star had left them behind. Soon, all that was left was the roar of the wind.

The cable hung straight down from the Jet Star, its end lost in the clouds.

Qualen backed away slowly. Travers watched him from the corner of his eye, not sure what he was going to do.

"Qualen!" Kristel yelled back. "We've got a problem."

He spoke quietly into the microphone. "No. Really?"

She shouted, "The jet—we're not leveling out."

"What's the matter?"

"I don't know."

Qualen looked from the pilot to the open door to the cable. He rushed forward.

"Get that cable up!" he said, pushing Kynette to his knees.

Reaching over the side, the young man began reeling in the cable. Ryan got behind to hold him. Travers and two other men, Heldon and the Englishman Delmar, stood there, watching.

"It's heavy!" Kynette shouted. "There's something on it—definitely something attached!"

Slowly, the end of the cable began emerging from the clouds. Looking over Kynette's shoulder, Travers could make out a dark form.

"The boxes are still there!" he said. "They're *there!*"

Qualen smiled and came over as the three cases came into view. But the smile vanished as they started swinging in long gentle arcs from the left to right.

"Hurry!" he said.

"I'm . . . doin' . . . my . . . fuckin' . . . *best!*" Kynette wheezed.

It struck Travers as funny that, standing by the open doorway, next to Kynette, attached to nothing, he wasn't as scared as he'd been when he had a safety line hooked to the cable. The plane was listing. If it listed a bit more, he could go sliding out. But the money was at stake. Money makes you brave. Money is worth the risk of dying. Besides, what else did he have? He couldn't very well go back to his job. He was supposed to be dead in the wreckage of the DC-9.

The Jet Star shuddered. Travers shot an anxious look toward the cockpit.

"*Kristel,*" Qualen hissed into the microphone.

"I *said* we've got problems! We must've taken some shrapnel somewhere."

The jolt sent the cable spinning in a circle.

Qualen looked down. "Get the cases in here, Kynette."

The young man started pulling faster. Travers bent beside him to help.

The plane dipped and lurched. The cable whipped up and the cases fell away. The catch opened.

"*No!*" Kynette screamed as he watched them tumble toward the ground.

The plane nosed down again. God or fate had decided to torment them now, given them a break in the clouds, let them watch as the boxes tumbled end over end, drifting apart, falling endlessly toward the peaks below.

Ryan punched the wall and walked over to the door. He looked at Qualen, who ordered the cable unhitched. As it followed the cases down, Qualen turned away. Ryan and Kynette shut the door.

The plane shuddered again and nosed down farther.

Qualen stood there, his blue eyes wide. They fastened on Travers and held him, like an eagle spotting prey.

"A foolproof plan, Travers?"

"It *was!*"

"If you'd sent the money first—"

"You'd be rich and I'd be dead! That just wasn't foolproof enough for *me.*"

Kristel interrupted. "Qualen!"

The tall man tore his eyes from Travers and headed for the cockpit. Everything in it was vibrating. He looked around. "Not good, I take it?"

The copilot was watching the altimeter. Kristel shook her head. She pointed to several gauges on her right. All of them were dropping.

"The hydraulics aren't functioning," she said. "Must've been shot up. I don't know."

"Bottom line?"

"I can't maintain altitude. We're going down."

Qualen looked out the window. The Jet Star was just

under the clouds now, and he could see the mountains below.

Qualen squeezed her shoulder. "Do what you can," he said, then leaned back to the cabin. "Crash positions!" he shouted, and headed for a seat to buckle himself into.

The six men sat and buckled themselves up.

"Hey, fuckhead," burly Heldon said to Travers. "I wouldn't buckle up if I was you. You may not want to survive this."

Travers pulled the belt tight, put his hands against the seat in front of him, and waited.

Fuck Heldon. Fuck Qualen. Fuck all of them.

He wanted to survive. Because he knew what Qualen did: draped around his neck was something that might yet save the day.

Assuming, of course, any of them were left to use it.

FOURTEEN

It was like flying a rock with wings.

Kristel didn't fight the Jet Star as it headed down at a forty-five-degree angle. Qualen said nothing as she let it drop, knew that the faster it got down the more hydraulic fluid they'd have left for any last-second maneuvers.

The speed of the descent pressed the passengers back in their seats.

Quick fall, and a quick death if Kristel couldn't stop it.

Qualen felt angry enough that he was sure he could pull the plane up by sheer force of will.

He told himself he shouldn't be mad at Travers. The guy was a government wage slave. Very little initiative, and even less imagination. Access was all he had. Access, and the monitor.

They were back in clouds, then through them, then down to three thousand–odd feet and in a blizzard.

He could dimly see a plateau ahead.

Kristel throttled up, leveled off slightly, banked toward it.

Two thousand four hundred feet. The plateau was only a thousand or so feet below, and they were coming up on it fast.

The copilot sat quietly, rigid with fear, as Kristel scanned the foliage, looking for—

"There!" she said, pointing with her forehead. "There's an opening!"

He saw it—a long, wide, sloping stretch between the trees. The ground wasn't level, and poking through the snow were rocks of different sizes. He looked beyond: five hundred yards past the clearing, the plateau ended. If they couldn't brake, they were going over the side.

The plane began to vibrate more intensely.

Kristel's teeth were locked. "Hold together, you bastard!"

She brought the nose up until they were level with the treetops, which clunked and thudded and scraped along the bottom of the plane.

Someone shouted something from the back, but his cry was drowned out as they hit the ground. The occupants were thrown forward as the plane hopped twice, skidded, and twisted as a wing clipped the trunk of a tree and stayed behind as the rest of the plane plowed ahead. Trees tore through the windows, buffeting the plane to the left and right.

It was a moment before Kristel had recovered from the impact and was able to play her last card, reversing what was left of the engines. They howled, though the flaps refused to come up.

"Come on, you son of a bitch!"

The second wing and the tail were shorn off as the plane hit a boulder. The fuselage was like a sled on an incline, out of control. It hit a tree stump, which tore through the cockpit, between the two seats, nearly taking Kristel's arm with it as it ripped off the right side of her seat. It continued to cut through the cabin, slicing up the right bank of seats as Ryan and Delmar jumped out of the way.

54

The noise was stupendous as the plane hit another tree, plowed past a scattering of rocks and trees, and finally came to rest with its nose dangling over the edge of the plateau, four thousand feet in the air.

Kristel released the controls, her hands shaking. She turned to the copilot, saw his face spattered with blood.

Dead.

Exhaling loudly, she lay back in what was left of her seat.

FIFTEEN

Brett frowned. Poised at the edge of a cliff, he scanned the sky, saw there were no thunderclouds to the east.

"Did you catch that thunder?"

Evan tapped the side of his crash helmet and cupped his hand to it.

"What?"

Brett yelled louder. "Did you catch the thunder?"

"Yeah. So?"

"It sounded like it came from behind us."

Evan looked back. "Sky's clear there."

"Yeah—"

"So no way, deadhead. Besides, it was too intense for thunder. Had to be a sonic boom, goon."

"From where? There isn't an airbase this side of the Springs."

Evan made a face. "So? Who the fuck cares, anyway? C'mon—let's rock an' roll!"

Brett shrugged, nodded, held his arms ahead of him like Superman, then jumped. Evan followed him by a heartbeat, the two of them soaring spread-eagled along the face of the cliff, hollering with delight, waiting until the last possible second to pull the ripcords on their backpacks and let their brightly colored parachutes stream out.

Whoo-whoo-whooing with excitement, they rode the chutes down, the thunder forgotten as the men played chicken, seeing who'd be the first to pull away from the fast-approaching treetops.

SIXTEEN

Travers was lying on his face, still belted in his seat. He was amazed at how still everything felt; after all the jostling and thudding, he savored the sudden unnatural calm.

His arms were folded under his chest, and he snaked one down to the belt. He popped it, dropped a few inches, and was relieved to feel no pain. He wiggled his feet, then moved his head from side to side, satisfied that he hadn't broken anything major.

With a start, he shoved a hand against his chest.

The case was intact. He sighed with relief. Turning to the left, he looked at Qualen.

The 9mm automatic scared Travers less than the internationally renowned lunatic's expression. It was too composed.

"You thought about everything," he said, his voice calm. "Did you expect what's happening now? Do you have a plan for me?"

Heldon limped up behind him, blood on his nose and forehead. He helped Delmar to his feet.

"Kill the pig," Heldon said. "His last fucking plan almost killed us!"

Travers kept his eyes on Qualen. "Kill me? You gave me your word. We're partners in this!"

"Were. You changed the plan; I changed the deal. Give me the tracking monitor."

"What the hell are you going to do with it?"

Kynette leaned close to his ear. "The monitor, asshole! Don't make him ask twice!"

"You're making a mistake," Travers told Qualen.

"Then it will make my second for today." He held out his hand.

Travers had watched Qualen's expression darken and knew it was time to fold the hand. He loosened his tie, undid his top two buttons, and slid the monitor from around his neck. He handed the case to Qualen, who opened it.

"Sure," Travers said, "take it. One thing, though. There are about fifty thousand code variations."

"I'll break your fucking neck!" Delmar said, hobbling forward.

Travers stepped back. "Go ahead, break my fucking neck. Go on! But in case anybody slept through the landing, you're going to need all the money you can find to buy your way out of this country. You know it and I know it."

Qualen looked from Travers to the monitor. He stared at the keypad, and at the raised screen above it.

"This round goes to you, Travers," Qualen said ominously.

Heldon hugged himself. His breath came in icy little puffs. "Boss—how're we gonna get off this mountain even if we do find the cash?"

Qualen allowed himself a satisfied smile. "That, at least, will not present a problem. Kristel, how are you doing?"

The pilot was bent over the instrument panel. She held up a screwdriver. "Almost ready."

SEVENTEEN

The rain had turned to snow in the foothills, and it fell heavily around the ranger cabin. The flakes were thick and accumulating quickly, the wind piling drifts against the cabin and the chopper.

Frank was finishing up his canvas, Hal had popped a movie in the VCR, and Jessie was reading a book.

"Who taped this?" Hal asked.

"I did," Frank said. "I like war movies."

"Me, too," said Hal. "I also like a plot. This thing's just—"

All three rangers were suddenly alert as the scanner radio crackled to life.

"Somebody help . . . please. . . . Is anybody there? . . . We need help. . . ."

Hal was closest to the desk and darted over. "Rocky Mountain Rescue, come in!"

"Please help. We're stranded."

"Do you know where you are?"

"No—we were hiking and lost our bearings. . . . We didn't expect this weather to come in so fast."

Frank had poked his brush in a tin of thinner and was already at the walk-in supply closet, pulling out the gear.

Jessie put the book aside and walked over to Hal.

"Can you identify yourselves?" Hal asked. "How many are there?"

"Oh, God—I'm scared!"

"It'll be okay, I promise. Just calm down and tell me how many members in your party?"

"Ummm . . . five people," she lied. "I don't know where we are. I only see something that looks like a . . . I don't know, a cylinder-type rock formation. Over."

Jessie said, "Got to be Comb Bluff."

"Shit," Frank said. "We'll need the chopper for that."

Hal nodded. "Ma'am—right now the winds are too strong to get a chopper up there."

"Oh no—"

"It'll be all right. Try to stay calm. We're on our way with supplies. You're going to be all right."

"Please hurry. Billy is going into shock. . . . We need insulin. . . . Please hurry, please. . . ."

The voice faded and then it was gone.

Hal turned up the volume, hit auto-tune, and watched the digital readout try to find the signal.

"Wait!" he shouted into the mike. "Come in. Do you read?"

There was only static. Hal hit the desk with the heel of his hand. "Damn! Lost contact."

Frank said, "That's okay. At least we know where they are."

"Right. Jess, you and Frank get the tents, thermal clothing, and medical supplies together."

"What are you going to do?"

"Bring them up."

"Who's going with you?"

"You're looking at him."

Jessie shook her head slowly. "That's dumb. What if the

61

storm hangs around for a few days? What then?"

He kissed her forehead. "This is what they pay us for, Jess. The first break in the weather, get up there as fast as that machine will fly."

He started toward the stack of items Frank had placed by the door. Jessie grabbed his arm.

"This is a two-person job, Hal. Two people minimum."

"There isn't anyone else, Jess." He leaned close. "You think I'm gonna haul Frank out there on foot?"

"Then I'll go."

"No way, Jessie. When was the last time you climbed in weather like this?"

"When was the last time *you* did?"

Hal looked at her. "I'll be all right."

"You think so. Hal, every opportunity you've had for the last year to maybe get yourself hurt, you just don't hesitate, do you?"

He gently removed her hand. "I appreciate your concern, but you're taking this a little too far, aren't you?"

"You tell me."

"I swear, Jessie. If I didn't think I could do it, I wouldn't— honest. Now, I've gotta run. We've got some sick and cold people out there."

Frank leaned from the closet. "I'm giving you a half dozen flares. That enough?"

"More than."

Jessie watched the flurry of activity, numb as Hal called out orders. After a minute, she turned away. "I still think you're crazy."

Hal smiled. "Now *that* may be true. Crazy, yes. Suicidal, no. I'll see you up there, okay?"

He looked back at Jessie. "I'll be okay—I promise." He smiled again and left, Jessie watching as he walked quickly toward the south. When he disappeared up the first hill, she ran to the door.

"Where you going?"

"Home, Frank."

"*Home*? What for?"

But Jessie didn't answer. Frank stood in the open door and watched as she climbed into the Jeep, swung away from the cabin, and headed back down the narrow road.

EIGHTEEN

Kristel leaned back, disconnecting wires from the battery in the cockpit.

Travers watched as Qualen leaned down and kissed her.

"We need insulin." Qualen smiled. Then he turned to Travers. "Would you have thought of that?"

Travers tensed. It wasn't bad enough that they were lost in the mountains with the money God knows where. He was going to have to put up with Qualen that much longer.

He did take solace in one thing, however. When the rangers arrived, they would be the ones taking the brunt of Qualen's anger, leaving him free to concentrate on the missing cases.

Travers stepped aside as Qualen returned to the cabin, joining him as he gathered the men around to plan the next move.

NINETEEN

The Jeep tore down the muddy mountain road to the main road, which was also muddy and rutted. Jessie didn't care. The wipers beat furiously across the window, rain pounded on the roof, and half the time Jessie couldn't see more than five yards in front of her.

She swerved to avoid a red fox, then raced ahead. All the while, she kept glancing to the left, looking for headlights.

This was the only road back to town. Gabe would have to have taken it. She only hoped that he'd been feeling nostalgic instead of pissed off. The former, and he'd still be there. The latter, and he'd be long gone.

She swung the Jeep onto the even muddier road by a sign that read, "Creature Comforts: A Development for People and Their Pets." She sped past the first two houses, shifted gears to get up the hill to her driveway, then floored the pedal.

"Yes!" she cheered when she saw the Land Rover. Gabe had just flipped up the tailgate and was pushing climbing gear inside. She skidded to a stop beside it, throwing mud, and pushed open the door.

"Gabe! Thank God you didn't leave."

Gabe looked at her. "What's wrong?"

"We just got an emergency call. Five climbers stranded off Comb Bluff. The weather's pouring in fast and Hal's gone up alone."

Gabe showed no expression. "Hal's a good climber. He knows what he's doing." His eyes fell and he headed back inside. Jessie followed him.

"Gabe, you know as well as I do that if he gets up there and gets socked in by the weather, they'll never make it down. He needs someone who has emergency medical training and knows every handhold on these peaks."

Gabe picked up his holdall.

"I'm the last person he wants help from—and besides, that's not what I came back here for."

"I know. But right now, our problems aren't the issue. Those people are. What if he can't do it alone? What about *their* lives?"

He shifted uncomfortably. "I don't know. You know how it is, Jess. I haven't climbed in months—you lose the feel."

"Maybe you mean the nerve."

Gabe's mouth closed tightly. He excused himself and started around her.

"Gabe, I'm sorry—I didn't mean that." She came a step closer. "You don't want to be responsible for anybody's life anymore. I understand and I sympathize. I really do. But I'm talking about somebody that was your best friend."

Gabe walked around her. He stopped in the doorway.

"Please, Gabe. He went up the west ridge. If you go up the south face, you can catch him, no problem."

Gabe hesitated, then continued out the door.

"Gabe!" Jessie ran after him. "Don't you feel anything anymore?"

"Feel anything? I came back for you, didn't I?"

"Not about me—feel anything about yourself. If you don't do this now, you're going to be stuck on that ledge for the rest of your life. Please, Gabe—if you won't do it for Hal or for me, do it for yourself."

Gabe looked at her, profound sorrow in his eyes. "See you around," he said quietly.

Jessie stood in the snow as he drove off, the drops washing away her tears as quickly as they formed.

TWENTY

Gabe left the driveway and hurried down the main road, fighting the bitterness and frustration that threatened to overwhelm him. He glanced over at the rearview mirror and saw an eighteen-wheeler bearing down on him—like the memories, inescapable. Gabe felt sick and his hands were shaking. He pulled off the road and let the truck roar past.

His left foot was pressing hard against the floor. He held the wheel so tightly his knuckles were white.

What the hell was he doing? Was he trying to spare Hal more pain or punish him? The guy hadn't said more than three words to him in the weeks after the accident. Apologies, dinner, football tickets, nothing budged him. If Hal had given him an inch, he'd've stayed. If he'd said, just once, *I know you did your best* or *I would've done the same thing*, they could have started again. It wouldn't have been easy, but it would have been doable. He didn't leave because of Jessie. He left because of Hal. Hal may not have been trying, but he succeeded in helping to pull him and Jessie apart. Maybe that didn't even things up, but it helped put him in an emotional shithole right next to Hal.

Gabe watched the wipers slash at the driving rain.

Do it for yourself....

Jessie's last words echoed in his head. She meant well, but she really didn't get it. He could pay off the national debt and cure cancer tomorrow, and it still wouldn't make up for what happened on the Tower. The scales didn't work that way. Unless he brought Sarah back to life, nothing would change.

Gabe put his forehead against the steering wheel. "So why the hell are you sitting here, jerkoff, instead of tear-assing back to Denver?"

That was really the question, and he knew the answer. The answer was, because forgetting everything else, never minding who the players were, there were people in trouble and he was—at one time, at least—uniquely suited to help.

Going out there was the right thing to do. He pounded the steering wheel and, throwing the car into gear, he U-turned hard, cursing himself and fate and offering a peremptory oath at any driver who dared to get in his way as he headed toward the south face of Comb Bluff.

TWENTY-ONE

Head Comptroller Walter Wright sat behind his desk, drumming on the rim of his Universal Studios *Miami Vice* mug, huffing as he thought about how Travers had played him like a banjo, wondering what golf trophy, framed photo, or hotsy-tot citation he should throw the mug at. He finally gave up and took a walk down the hall, trying to think things through.

He'd often wondered if he had it in him to kill a person. Now he knew. The final *Jeopardy* answer was Richard Travers. Travers had been distracted these last few weeks, and had asked for this assignment, said he needed some time shuttling back and forth, rote stuff, to get his head together. Wright had given it to him, hoping it'd help get him over whatever was bothering him—and the man screws up. Loses a plane. And other agents. And one hundred million bucks.

What the hell could Travers have been thinking? He was supposed to check the condition of the plane personally, examine all weather conditions, search everyone who came on board—

As Wright joined the heavy flow of traffic down the main

concourse connecting one building to the next, Agent Davis spotted him and ran to catch up.

Davis cleared his throat. "Sorry. This was late."

"Okay," Wright said. "What's the report? Where the hell is that plane?"

Davis studied the fax. "Mike Quirk at the tower says there's no radio contact at all, sir. And Communications says we're not receiving the tracer signal from the cockpit's flight recorder."

"Meaning it went down."

"We have to assume it did, sir—in the storm. That storm front, by the way, is still building. Even if we could get a search plane up now, it'd be impossible to see anything on the ground."

"Where're we talking about?"

Davis pulled a map from under his arm and pointed to a circled area. "According to the flight plan, they'd have been somewhere over these mountains—hundreds of square miles of miserable terrain."

"Okay. No air search. What about the roads?"

"Most of this area doesn't even *have* roads. And the way it's been snowing there, what roads there are may already be impassable."

Wright's secretary Linda popped from the crowd with two serious-looking men in tow. "Mr. Wright, there are two FBI agents who would like to speak with you."

"Why am I not surprised?" he said, tight-lipped.

Linda motioned the men over, and they fell into step with Wright as he continued along, Davis dogging the group. Both men were tall; one held a leather portfolio under his arm.

The stockier of the two men said, "Mr. Wright, I'm Agent Hayes and this is Agent Michaels. We're here about the disappearance."

"Look, gentlemen, if you're concerned about the agent who was along for the ride—"

"Matheson wasn't just along for the ride," Hayes said. "He was working surveillance."

Wright stared from one man to the other. His brow knit. "Surveillance. For what?"

"The Bureau had been receiving sketchy reports about Treasury flight patterns being monitored from Denver to San Francisco."

"By whom?"

"Please, sir," Michaels said. "We'll get to that."

"It was thought best," continued Hayes, "not to alert anyone in your department in case there was the possibility of it being an inside job."

Wright waved his hand. "That's impossible. You suggest a hijacking? Impossible. Not only did I have my best men on that flight, each one of those cases are monitored, and the money is in unexchangeable denominations. It would be useless for anyone to steal."

Michaels opened the portfolio he was carrying and presented a folder to Wright. "Not for this man, Mr. Wright."

Wright opened it and looked at the fuzzy eight-by-ten on top. "Who the hell is this?"

"Eric Qualen. He's the one we've been tracking without much success. He's a former member of military intelligence who found it more profitable going to the other side. Industrial hijacking from South Africa, theft and disposal of millions in negotiable bearer bonds, you name it. He's got the international connections to move this currency, and one hundred million dollars offers one hell of a temptation to this psychotic."

Wright ran a finger down Qualen's dossier. "Jesus Christ, this can't be happening. And you think he was involved somehow?"

"We do."

Hayes said, "As we said, he probably had someone on the inside. That's what Matheson was trying to find out. What we need from you is a complete profile on all the men aboard the jet, backgrounds both business and personal. If any of them was involved, and we can intercept them—"

"Gotcha," Wright said. "Davis, arrange it."

Davis said he would and hurried past the FBI men.

Michaels and Hayes followed from a distance.

Wright continued to study the dossier, taking in the facts and figures of Qualen's life. As he did so, one thing stood out.

Qualen had been in Cuba, in Iraq, in Haiti, in Somalia, and in the Philippines—and in most of those places, his "eliminations" were in the double digits. Some of them our guys. He'd worked for terrorists, radicals, anyone with a checkbook bigger than someone else's.

If he had somehow gotten ahold of the plane and the money, one thing was damn sure: getting it back wasn't going to be easy.

TWENTY-TWO

The fifteen-hundred-foot south wall of Comb Bluff was just that: a wall, straight up and down, with the kind of handholds that give daredevils pause, with overhangs that don't forgive mistakes.

Gabe had rigged a stirrup with pitons and was clambering up the side of one of the larger overhangs.

" . . . and if you go up the south wall," he said as he worked his way up the small, makeshift ladder, "you can catch him, no problem."

The wind was ferocious and the snow-covered rock made the going slippery and slow. Worse was the fact that the higher he went, the more slippery the climb became, the rain having frozen to create a coat of ice.

He made it to the top of the nob of rock and reached behind him to reel in the stirrup. As he did so, he looked down. It was a sheer drop of seven hundred feet, and he felt a wave of insecurity.

He shut his eyes and put his face to the cold rock.

Insecurity. That was something new for him. It was what Sarah must have felt—

No! Don't think like that!

Gabe opened his eyes. "Keep going," he told himself. "Just keep going."

Keep plugging ahead and don't look back. Don't look back at *anything*. He looked up. Just a few hundred feet to go.

He pulled the bolt gun from his belt. Aiming ahead, he fired, rigged a new line, and continued upward.

The rest of the climb went a little easier—Gabe hustled to show himself he still could. You could fall off a step and break your skull; this was a higher step, was all. You shoot, tie the line, climb. Don't hesitate, don't think, just *do*.

The first part of the climb had taken over an hour; the last part took less than half that. He felt a sense of satisfaction as he pulled himself over the top, breathing hard but standing, ready to face the bigger problem just ahead.

TWENTY-THREE

Gabe heard Hal grunting.

After reaching the top, Gabe had hiked over to the top of the west ridge—a longer, gentler slope that made sense for a guy carrying supplies—and sat against a boulder, waiting just out of sight. He didn't want Hal pulling himself over the edge, seeing him, and letting go. That was the kind of news that wouldn't play really well back at the ranger station.

He listened as Hal muttered about the weight of the pack, bitched about a scraped something-or-other, and thanked the weather for starting to clear.

It sounded a lot like the old Hal, his friend. Against all reason, Gabe hoped that time might have started to heal the wounds, that they could at least talk.

With a clank of gear, Hal came forward. Gabe rose and stepped around the boulder.

"Morning, Hal."

Hal saw him and stopped. His expression went from blank to surprise to disgust in the time it took him to draw a breath.

"What the hell are you doing here?!"

"I was with Jessie. She filled me in."

"Did she?" Hal punched his open glove. "Great. Just—great. Now let *me* fill you in. You can get your ass back down an' go back to whatever hole you been hiding in—"

"When we get this group down, I'm gone."

"You're gone *now*! I don't climb with people I can't trust. Why'd you come up, to prove something?"

"I'm here for the same reason you are," Gabe said quietly, "so let's just do it, okay?"

"No, I don't think that's right. I'm here to do my job. You're here because you can't pass up another chance to play hero."

"Look, Hal—"

"My name is for my friends, mister."

Gabe sighed. "I know what you think, what you're feeling—"

Hal started toward him. "You don't know anything. Want proof? You thought you *knew* what to do on the Tower. Well, we did it your way and Sarah died."

"If I could've taken her place, I would have. I did what I thought was right."

"Well, you were *wrong*." Hal was just a few feet away now, and was jabbing ahead with his index finger. "It was your weight on the line that did it—"

"That's not true."

"It was you playing hero instead of doing it by the book."

"There wasn't time for anything else."

Hal stopped. He was breathing heavily, his face almost in Gabe's. "We'll never know, will we? And since there's no bringing her back, why don't you crawl off somewhere."

Hal stalked past Gabe, toward the slope that headed to the Bluff.

Gabe watched him go. "Don't you think it's been bad for me too? It was a bad time for everybody."

Hal spun. "What the hell do *you* know about a bad time?" He stormed back, arms flailing. "You didn't love her! You didn't have to explain to her family!"

"And you weren't looking into her eyes when she fell. Now, drop it!"

With a cry, Hal grabbed Gabe, catching him off-guard and pushing him toward the ledge. His fingers were wrapped tightly around the front of Gabe's jacket.

"No, buddy! It was *you* who dropped it!"

Hal had Gabe so that he was off-balance, the weight of his backpack pulling him over, the heels of his boots hanging off the ledge.

Hal was growling, his neck taut, nostrils flared, hands shaking. "For half my life I've wanted *you* on that ledge, hanging by your goddamn fingernails, begging me for help. I've wanted to watch you slip away slowly, like she did. I've wanted to see you *fall*."

Gabe's eyes were sad, his face relaxed. "If you want, do it. I don't care."

Hal continued to glare at him for a long moment, then pulled him back in. His gaze was withering.

"Yeah, man, I want it. I've wanted to see you fly more than I've ever wanted anything in my life. But not that way. Not askin' for it. When this thing's over, it's you and me— back on the ledge."

"I won't fight you."

"You'll fight," Hal said, stalking toward his gear. "You'll fight because I'll remind you how you choked for Sarah, and then you choked for Jessie. You'll fight or you'll jump off the fucking cliff, because those are the only ways you're gonna get away from me."

Hal grabbed the backpack without stopping, slipping it on as he started toward the cloud-covered bluff.

The sun had vanished and it started to sleet. But Gabe didn't feel it as he started after Hal. All he felt was the devastating sadness of failure, of having reached out his hand again and failing to pull in a friend.

TWENTY-FOUR

"They're here!"

Ryan was looking through the binoculars, watching the foot of the bluff. He followed the two figures as they stopped talking and crossed the top of the lower bluff, dwarfed by the mountains and wicked clouds to the south. They started climbing the slope, hand over hand, the man who was behind quickly overtaking the man who was in front.

"Boss? You copy? I said they're here."

"I copy," Qualen said. "We have guests."

Ryan heard fumbling on the earphones. Qualen was probably boffing Kristel again. He bet she was due for more than the million-five cut each of the rest of them had been promised.

No matter. He could be happy with his share. Pay off some gambling debts, buy a Jag, hit the road for a few years.

Ryan removed the headset and stuffed it in his backpack, then unzipped his coat to the middle and leaned against a tree. He used his coat cuff to wipe snow from the glasses, then looked at the wreck, trying to peer into the cabin. It was too dark, but Qualen had to be banging her. When someone pissed him off like Travers had, sex or killing was the only thing that made him feel better. And he couldn't kill anyone.

Not yet, anyway.

TWENTY-FIVE

Gabe had resisted offering Hal a helping hand until they were near the very top of the slope. They hadn't needed their picks or rope; the angle wasn't bad, and there were enough handholds. But Hal was carrying all the rescue gear, and he had some trouble with the loose rocks on top.

They were about two hundred yards up, some four yards from the top. Hal was breathing hard, right below Gabe, and was having a tough time pulling himself up.

"I'm going up," Gabe said. "Need a hand?"

"Don't bother," Hal said.

Hal pulled himself to the top of the bluff and joined Gabe.

They were puzzled by what they saw. Even through the sleet, they could see the sheared trees, the gouged terrain, the distant wreck of the airplane.

Gabe tapped Hal on the shoulder and pointed. Hal rose and looked. Then the two looked at Ryan and Heldon, both of them pointing automatic machine pistols.

"I think we've been had," Gabe said.

"Walk," Ryan said, motioning with the gun, then stepping back with Heldon, keeping their distance as the men passed.

The hike to the wreckage was short, Hal muttering angrily, Gabe stealing looks back, hoping the gunmen might slip on the sleet-slickened rocks and hard snow. They were only about ten feet behind them—well within range of the bolt gun hooked to Gabe's belt.

But the men didn't falter. When they reached the plane, Qualen, Travers and the others were waiting, snow swirling around them.

"Good of you to come," Qualen said. "But where's the helicopter?"

Hal stepped forward, over debris. "What the hell's going on here?"

Qualen slammed Gabe into the fuselage. Gabe went for the attacker, but Delmar grabbed him from behind.

Gabe understood that they were at a disadvantage, and exchanged a quick look with Hal. They were going to have to buy some time.

Qualen's eyes shifted to Gabe. "Where's the chopper?"

"It can't fly in this weather."

"Either one of you chopper pilots?"

"No." Gabe looked at Hal.

Travers stepped forward. "You're both with the mountain rescue team?"

"Yeah," Hal said.

"Anyone else following?"

Hal shook his head.

"What're your names?"

"Tucker and Walker."

Travers stood between the rangers and Qualen. If he'd been here alone, Gabe would have pushed him into the boss and bolted from the fuselage. But for the first time in months, he wasn't alone. He wished he was in the mood to appreciate the irony.

"Tucker and Walker," Travers said, "we've lost three cases."

Qualen said, "You know—suits, pants, socks, one hundred million dollars . . . the usual. But Travers was clever enough to bring along a tracking device."

"Don't use my name!" Travers snapped.

Gabe saw the boss's mood shift, the mock-courtliness gone and something volcanic just below the surface. The man didn't let it out, but it was there, hot and waiting.

Qualen looked at Gabe. "Inside," he said, picking up the gun and pointing.

Delmar pushed Hal and Gabe into the broken and buckled fuselage. Gabe saw a woman holding a map. Qualen motioned for Hal and Gabe to look at it.

"Key it," Qualen told Travers.

The agent elbowed past Ryan, stepped into the cabin, and began punching numbers into the monitor. Gabe watched as a display on top lit up with pulsing dots. Numbers appeared corresponding to a relief outline of a section of the mountain range.

"Look at the map, then at the monitor," Qualen said, walking up behind the men. "Recognize these locations?"

Gabe and Hal looked at each other, then back at the map. Neither man said a word.

"I saw that look of boy-scout ethics pass between you," Qualen said. "Say as little as possible, do as little as necessary to help the big, bad crook. I respect that. But let me perhaps *jar* your memory a little," Qualen said dryly. "You see, if you don't recognize them, you're useless. And useless items are always discarded. Right, Travers?"

Travers pounded the wall once. "Get off my back, Qualen!"

"Off? Agent Travers, I haven't got on it yet!"

Qualen leaned between Hal and Gabe, looking down with them, resting an arm on each man's shoulder. Gabe got the arm with the gun. He felt Qualen's thumb move, heard the hammer click.

"Now, then," Qualen said into Gabe's ear, "do you recognize the locations?"

Gabe nodded.

Qualen smiled. "That's good. Let's go."

TWENTY-SIX

The mountain wall sloped up at a forty-five-degree angle, with ledges jutting out every two yards or so. The wind howled and the sleet had become snow, both whirling furiously around the line of men moving up the peak.

Gabe and Hal were in the lead, with Qualen bringing up the rear. Gabe hammered in pitons as he ascended, using carabiner clips to create a guide rope; behind them, Kynette, Delmar, Heldon, Kristel and Ryan waited impatiently, Travers nervously.

Qualen seemed to be enjoying himself.

"The faster you find the cash, boys, the bigger the finder's fee!" he yelled.

The temperature fell and weather worsened as they continued climbing the peak, Gabe keeping up the pace just to make his captors' lives miserable. Their destination was Eagle Point, a large ledge below the area where the monitor said the first of the boxes was.

The climbing became easier when they reached a two-foot-wide ledge that wrapped around the top of the peak, like a soft ice-cream swirl.

As they reached the Point, Hal's walkie-talkie crackled on. Qualen pulled it from his belt.

"Hal, come in, please. Hal, are you there?"

Qualen flicked it off. "Which one of you is Hal?"

Hal stepped over.

"She sounds nice. Girlfriend?"

"No."

"Poor, poor boy scout. All right, Hal. You stay. You," he pointed to Gabe, "go and fetch."

"He doesn't know this mountain like I do," Hal said.

"Then he'll learn fast," said Qualen.

Delmar held a gun on Hal as he helped Gabe put on his crampons. "Handholds'll be slippery," Hal said, "and watch yourself under that overhang." He pointed to a section of the cliff over one hundred feet directly above them. "It could deliver anytime."

Gabe looked up. Hal was right. It was held to the mountain with spit. One good kick would send it crashing down.

Kynette gave Hal a shove. "Anytime you feel like sayin' something—don't. *Deliver* means give way, right?" He pulled a gun and pushed it under Gabe's chin. "You come closer than a three-point shot to that ledge, I'll deliver *this* up yer ass."

Qualen gestured impatiently. "All right now, friend of Hal, go on. Fetch."

"I need the bolt gun and ice axe."

"Don't give him anything!" Kynette said.

"You heard my secretary of defense."

"And for insurance," Travers said, "take his coat."

"Christ!" Hal said. "He'll freeze to death."

"You've got your own problems, Hal," Qualen said, "such as the fact that you annoy me a great deal. People who annoy me have a habit of lowering the nation's mean life expectancy." He looked back at Gabe. "The coat, please."

Gabe removed it, handed it to him.

"Empty your backpack. You'll need the space."

Gabe undid the zipper, dumped the ropes, spare pitons, chocks and nuts, and ice hammer onto the ledge.

Qualen grinned and looked at Hal. "Now, Ryan, get me a rope. I want this dog on a leash."

Gabe looked up. This was going to be difficult, even for him.

Hal turned quickly to Gabe and whispered, "Forget me. If you can, get away."

"Would you?" Gabe asked as Ryan and Kynette pushed Hal to one side.

As the men put a noose around Gabe's leg, Qualen looked at him. "I like you, Walker. Your first name is . . . ?"

"Gabe."

"Gabriel. Like the angel. Well, let's hope you can fly, Gabriel, because if you're not back within, say, sixty minutes, not only will you be a lovely teal blue, but we'll see if your friend can fly—off the side of this ledge."

Gabe said nothing: he simply turned to the wall, looked for a handhold, and started up.

Though Hal was lying—Gabe knew the cliff better than he did—he was right about how slippery it was. Gabe had always made a habit of climbing barehanded on nice days, to toughen his fingertips; even so, it was difficult to find anything to hold onto.

Fifty feet up, there were no outcroppings, only cracks; pausing, trying not to tense, so he wouldn't shiver, Gabe removed his necklace—a necklace Jessie had given him after his little adventure in the Berkshires.

He heard Qualen yell, "Hey! What are you doing up there?"

He heard Hal answer, "The best he can, since you gave him nothing."

His friend was back, and that made the cold seem less than it was.

He dug his fingers into an icy crack overhead. Spotting a handhold well above he tugged himself up, muscles straining, hurting.

Pulling hard, he brought himself up and found a place to park his heels, dig in the crampons, on lumps of ice no bigger than his fist. He rested there for a moment, breathing hard, shaking out his shoulders. The rope, now fifty feet long, added five pounds to his weight.

Don't think—just do!

He looked for another crack, found one, and pulled himself to the next handhold. Then again. And again. And then he reached his hands over the top, found a frozen root sticking from the ground, and pulled himself up. As soon as he was off the face of the cliff, he fell on his back, exhausted. He turned his face to the right, looked down, and saw the men on the ledge looking up at him through the sleet. One of them gestured for him to get up.

Though the cold felt good on his sweating back, Gabe took a deep breath, sat up, and climbed to his feet. He leaned against a boulder and looked out across the snow-swept expanse. Under the snow, partly exposed, was what looked like a case.

The object was matte black, about two and a half feet by one and a half feet, battered, a busted red light on top, with snow collected in the dents. He got on his hands and knees, put his left hand against the opposite side of the crevasse for support, reached under the box, and pulled. It came free without a struggle, and he set it down in the snow. He grabbed a good-size rock, slamming it against the battered locks. They broke free and the case opened.

Gabe whistled as he looked down and ran his fingers across the neatly wrapped bills.

"Jesus."

He felt a tug on the rope. Shutting the case, he started back toward the rock wall away from the ledge.

TWENTY-SEVEN

Travers was standing near the edge of the cliff, looking up, looking at his watch, wiping snow from his bald head.

"I don't trust him."

"Why not?" Ryan said. "He can't cash the bills."

"No, but he can cash in. He can get help, be a hero, be on TV."

Qualen looked at Hal, who was standing even farther back, looking up. "You know him, Mr. Tucker. Will he run?"

Hal suddenly felt ashamed. He felt ashamed for everything he'd said and done over the last eight months. "Not Gabe," he said. "Gabe Walker doesn't run."

"No, I didn't think so," Qualen said.

Hal's face was turned up, but he watched as Qualen moved over to where Kynette was standing, the taut rope in his hand. Hal cocked his head slightly to the side, strained to hear.

"I don't think we need two guides," Qualen said, "especially if one of them is fearless. Retire Mr. Walker when he gets down."

Hal looked back up, showing no emotion. He waited—waited until Gabe appeared on the ledge. Waited until all of the men were looking up. Then he bolted forward.

"Gabe, don't come down! They're gonna kill you! *Don't come down!*"

Delmar was standing closest to Hal and dropped him with a forearm to the back of the neck. He put a boot on the ranger's arm, pinning him.

"You'll die instead, you fuck!" Delmar snarled.

"Pull the rope!" Qualen yelled to Ryan.

Ryan stood on the coil and began to wind it in.

"You can't help me!" Hal yelled. "Don't be a—"

Qualen spun and kicked him in the mouth.

"If you think you've nothing to lose, Mr. Tucker, think again. I can find family and friends." He held up the walkie-talkie. "Another word and you'll watch as *she* dies most grotesquely."

Hal lay there, tasting blood and ice, watching through bleary eyes as Ryan pulled on the rope.

"It's stuck!" Ryan yelled. "Something's wrong."

Hal smiled. "Go for it, Gabe," he said into the snow. "Kick some ass for me."

TWENTY-EIGHT

When Gabe heard Hal yell, he stopped and listened. He couldn't make out the first part, but the last few words were clear as a boom box: *Don't come down.*

As he stood there, he saw the slack in the rope begin to tighten. They were reeling him in.

That didn't make sense. He had at least twenty-five minutes left, more than enough time to get down, and he really thought Qualen trusted him. Something must have made him nervous. Or confident. Or suddenly cautious.

Gabe ran to the ledge before he was pulled there. He looked down.

He saw Hal lying on the ground, very still, with what looked like blood on his face. Gabe didn't know if he were alive or dead, but seeing Hal lying there brought home the fact that once they had the money and the chopper, not just he and Hal but also Frank and Jessie were going to be left here for some museum of the future to find.

The rope tightened and pulled his feet out from under him. Gabe flopped onto his back, grabbed the rope, drove his spiked heels into the ground, and pulled.

He slowed but didn't stop. The edge of the cliff was just five feet away. The edges of the box dug into Gabe's spine, but the pain gave him strength. He peered ahead, scuttled on his butt toward a big rock near the ledge, drove the heel of his leashed foot against it, then brought the other foot around and tried to slice the rope with a crampon.

The rope began to fray. He hammered his elbows down hard at his sides, into the icy ground, and managed to slow himself a little without destroying his funny bone. He heard Travers yelling, "Kynette, help him! Pull, goddammit!"

"Rupture yourself," Gabe grunted.

He angled his tied foot so that the rope was lying on the rock. Then he ripped the crampon from his other foot and began slashing and pounding at the rope. It wasn't pretty, but the rope came apart more quickly. He pulled his leg toward himself, straining the rope and his thigh muscles both.

A sudden hard tug caused him to lose his grip and pinwheel toward the edge, his head and shoulders going over.

"Shoot, Heldon!" Travers yelled. "What the hell are you waiting for!"

Bullets chewed up the cliff just below. Gabe reached to the right and swung himself counterclockwise so his feet were once again facing the ledge, and slamming his leashed heel on the very edge of the cliff, he sat up, grabbed his leash, pulled hard, and sawed with a crampon.

The rope snapped and Gabe slid back nearly a yard.

"You fucking idiots!" Travers yelled. "Walker! Walker, you bring down the money or your friend's dead!"

"We can't and he knows it, agent!" snapped Qualen.

Frustrated, Travers shoved Hal aside. "Get him!"

Gabe went back to the case, and held a fistful of banded bills over the side. "I want to talk to him or I'm gonna throw your fucking money over the fucking cliff, a bundle at a time."

"I hear you," Qualen said. "Sit tight."

Gabe inched ahead and looked over the ledge. He saw two of the men picking Hal up. A third fired at Gabe, who pulled in the backpack.

"Stop shooting!" Qualen shouted. "All right, Mr. Walker. Reach out and touch someone."

"Hal?"

"Yeah. I'm okay, Gabe. How are you?"

"On top of things. Can you climb?"

"I—I can climb."

"Okay. Qualen?"

"Right here."

"We're gonna do some swapping. You send him up, I bring the box down."

"No can do, Mr. Walker. I need a guide."

"You've got me. When I come down with the box, I stay."

Hal yelled, "Gabe, they don't want you! They're afraid of—"

Gabe heard Hal groan and looked over, saw him flat on his back, holding his gut, one of the men standing next to him.

Qualen was looking up and motioning to the men. "Get him!"

Gabe saw one of them reach for his bolt gun. He doubted they had much experience, but that didn't matter: with the gun and stirrups, a few of them would make it up, and quickly. He had to slow them down.

Hal began to crawl to the right. Good man. He knew the score.

Scampering to the left, Gabe put the box down and stood over the ledge Hal had been pointing to earlier. He put his foot against a loose boulder and leaned over. Heldon saw him and fired, as Gabe had expected. As the bullets tore at the ledge, then at his feet, the rumble of the inevitable avalanche began, raining snow and rock on the men, wiping Heldon off the side, drowning his scream in its thunder, and sending the other men scurrying for the relative safety of the cliff face.

Hal had made it to the other side of the lower ledge, clear of the bulk of the cascading ice and earth.

But the mountain was just getting started. As the roar echoed around him, Gabe heard, then felt, the peak above begin to rumble. He looked up and saw powder rise from the deep snow overhead. Snowball-sized chunks began to break away, picking up more snow as they fell and kicking other pieces loose.

Suddenly, the entire mountainside began to slide; pelted with snow, Gabe grabbed the case and took cover under an overhang as the snow crashed around him, deafening and relentless. As the avalanche poured over him and spilled down the crevasse, he heaved the case into the cascade. It hit the rocky ledge and split open, spilling cash, the green mixing with the white snow. As the thieves watched, Heldon finally disappeared in the crush of ice.

Gabe had no idea how long the avalanche lasted; when it was man versus mountain, every instant seemed like a lifetime.

When it finally stopped, he shook the snow off his head, put his hand over the top of the fissure, and crawled from his sanctuary, numb and battered but alive.

TWENTY-NINE

As the last of the snow skidded from the Point and fell past the ledge, Qualen stepped back from the mountainside.

And saw some of the bills lying at his feet, many more fluttering through the air, but most of them sailing on the currents beneath the ledge, carried off in three directions over dozens of square miles.

Eyes blazing, Qualen stalked through the knee-deep snow to where Hal lay huddled in a corner of the ledge. While his men scooped up whatever money was lying about, Qualen reached down and grabbed the ranger by the throat.

"Your friend thought he was being smart and ended up buying himself the most expensive funeral in history. Now it's just you. Step out of line just once, and it'll be recreation time with you, me, and the bolt gun."

The walkie-talkie hummed on.

"Come in, Rescue Unit, over. Rescue Unit—what's going on, Hal?"

Qualen pulled his 9mm from his jacket and pushed it to Hal's temple, then handed him the walkie-talkie. "I need time, so you talk. No tricks, no codes, no messages. You haven't found us. It was a fake call."

Hal spit blood. He switched on the unit.

"Jessie, I reached the top of the Tower. So far, no sign of anyone. Looks like a phony call. Over."

There was a short silence.

"You gotta be kidding me!" Jessie said. "A ham with too much time on her hands, I'll bet. Do you want me to fly up after you? Over."

"Negative, Jess. It's snowing and the winds are too high. I'm going to ride out the storm here. I'll take shelter in the old—"

Qualen pulled the walkie-talkie from Hal's mouth.

"Nice try. You don't know where you're going to take shelter."

Hal yanked his hand away. "Sorry, Jess. Dropped the radio. I'll find shelter nearby. Or else I've got the mini-tent. Over and out."

He clicked the unit off. Qualen pulled it away, then backhanded the ranger across the cheek.

"Don't ever pull away from me again."

"Qualen!" Travers was trudging over, a thin stack of bills in one hand, the monitor in the other. "What's wrong with you? Why the hell don't you have her come up?"

Hal snickered. "Sure. Have her come up. You people from the city know a lot about downdrafts. They have a way of wiping out choppers. And it's the only one. If the Huey goes down, you go nowhere. They'll be chiseling your face off this ice wall next spring." He looked up at Qualen. "Your call."

Qualen looked from Hal to the monitor. "Let's go to the next case."

Delmar shoved Hal forward and the group moved out.

They reached a small river and crossed it in the whipping snow. Travers showed Hal the monitor; the next blip was above, almost straight up.

"Where is this?" Qualen asked.

Hal motioned to a wooded area ahead. "On top of the peak."

"How much climbing is involved?"

"Not much. Slope's a grade one, thirty-five-, forty-degree incline."

Travers was suspicious. He got the binoculars from Ryan and looked up. "It looks like a long and winding route. Is it the only one?"

Hal said, "No."

"Meaning?" Qualen demanded.

"Meaning if you got balls that clang, there's a faster way up the East Face . . . only it's smooth as glass, five thousand feet by five thousand feet. Maybe a dozen guys in the world could do it in good weather. Only a psycho would try it in a storm."

"We can walk to the other one from here?"

Hal nodded.

"Then let's go," Qualen said to the others. "Let's make ourselves richer by two cases or poorer by one ranger."

99

THIRTY

Jessie was sitting in the swivel chair, looking out at the snow piled up outside. Bracketed to the outside wall, the windspeed gauge was spinning faster than she'd ever seen it go.

Frank was standing beside her, his hands in his pockets.

"I don't like it," Jessie said. "Hal said the Tower, but he's on Comb Bluff."

"So? It was a slip of the tongue. He made a long trek and he's cold."

"I don't think so."

Frank tapped a book lying on the desk. "And I think you've been reading too many thrillers."

"Really?" She cocked a thumb toward the closet. "What did Hal take?"

"Flares, blankets, two thermal suits, and his gear."

"No tent."

Frank looked back. "I'll be damned. You're right. So why'd he tell us he had one?"

Jessie stood, got her slicker. "Something's wrong up there. I want you to fly me to the west valley."

"Out of the question."

"Frank, the winds are never too strong there, and it's only a half-hour climb to the Douglas Shaft. That's the only shelter for miles around—Hal would have to go there."

Frank rubbed the back of his neck. "I don't know."

"Look, if I don't link up with him, you can come and pick me up by nightfall." She offered her hand. "Deal?"

Frank looked at the hand. "Hal will have my head for this."

"And it's such a handsome head." Jessie hurried toward the door.

Frank didn't.

She stopped beside his easel and tapped it. "Come on, Frank. Do this for me and I swear I'll buy one of your paintings."

"And display it?"

"Right over the fireplace," she said.

Frank smiled and started after her. "I admit it—I *can* be bought." Pulling on his parka, he followed her into the snow.

The trip was rockier than Jessie had expected, but not as bad as some clear-weather flights. That was one of the first things she had learned during flight training: never judge a day by sunshine. Hot sun could do more to stir up the air than a cold Arctic wind.

As Frank piloted the craft along the foothills and up toward the higher elevations, Jessie connected the harness to the winch.

She still felt a cold chill whenever she picked up the harness. Just seeing it whisked her back to that awful day.

But she forged ahead. As she'd told Gabe and Hal so many times, what else was there to do?

Thinking of Gabe brought her down even more. Maybe she didn't know him as well as she thought; she could've sworn he'd agree to rendezvous with Hal. Give it one last shot, do it out of devotion to Hal or to her or from a sense of duty . . . *something.*

But maybe this Gabe wasn't the same man who'd forced himself to go out alone to recover Sarah's body. Maybe too much time had passed, too much pain had numbed him. God knew it had changed Hal.

"You almost ready back there?"

Jessie started pulling on the harness. "Just about."

"We're almost there. Now, you're *sure* you want to do this?"

"You mean buy *Banana Eating a Monkey*?"

Frank's mouth twisted. "You know darn well what I mean."

"I'm sure," she said.

Five minutes later, with the Huey Ranger on autopilot and hovering over a flat expanse in the west valley, Frank was lowering Jessie to the ground. Despite the buffeting winds and rain, the drop went without a hitch; disconnecting herself and waving that she was okay, Jessie started toward the west.

Two minutes after that, her walkie-talkie came on.

"Jessie? Jessie, you copy? Over."

"I copy, Frank. Over."

"Jessie, I'm coming back for you. Weather stat just radioed with an update. They're calling for wind gusts of up to fifty knots for tonight. Over."

"Don't worry. If you can't make it back, I'll hole up at the Douglas Shaft. Over."

"Alone? Over."

"Stop worrying, Frank. You sound like a mother hen. Over."

"Rooster! Forget the hen stuff. Listen, you just be safe, honey. Over and out."

Jessie stopped to tie the laces of her hood, then continued into the dark afternoon, the howling wind swallowing up the distant sound of the chopper and making her feel very much alone.

THIRTY-ONE

Two years before, Hal had nicknamed the East Face "Mountaineering's Five Hundred Club," inspired by baseball's exclusive club of batters who had hit five hundred or more career home runs. There weren't a lot of players who had done that . . . and there weren't a lot of climbers who had taken the East Face. In the thirty years the ranger station had been operating, only five people had done it—and none of them ever went after it a second time.

Gabe had climbed it his first week on the job, as soon as his disability insurance had been okayed. Upon reaching the top, he told Hal that it would be a cold day in hell before he did it again. It wasn't just that the sheer rock face itself was difficult, spray from the thirty-yard-wide waterfall was cold and, depending which way the wind blew, it could be blinding. During winter, the droplets froze on the rock so that what were once handholds were slippery lumps no good to the climber.

Gabe guessed that where he was, three thousand feet up the Face, with wind chill factored in, it was at least twenty degrees below zero. And when he had paused to rest briefly at the halfway point, he wondered if maybe this *was* hell.

He certainly couldn't think of a less appealing place on the planet.

This was his hell, punishment for his myriad sins. But it was the only way to reach those other spots on the monitor before Qualen and his band.

Now, after two hours on the East Face, Gabe was shaking violently from the cold and from the strain; right now, a coat would have meant more to him than the other two boxes of money. The insides of his arms were numb, the insides of his pants were brittle with ice, and the only thing that kept him going was the knowledge that if he didn't head Qualen's party off somewhere, somehow, Hal and Jessie would probably die. The prospect of maybe getting to punch Qualen's smug face through the back of his skull also held some appeal. He had to admit, though, that if it weren't for the blue-white pillars of ice that spotted the Face, he wouldn't have gotten even this far. Each year, runoff from melting snows froze in massive columns, columns he was able to straddle, in which he was able to dig his crampons. Columns that provided him with upward mobility where the rock wall did not.

He went up, increasingly just inches at a time, heading toward a serac, a chandelier of ice, the mouth of the frozen waterfall. The top section of the Face sloped outward, and though the climb was doable with equipment, he'd never make it with just his bare hands. He had to go for the icicles, which—with luck and a little ingenuity—he felt he could climb.

It was an hour before he reached it, a mass of ice that curled over the waterfall like ice cream on a cone. Despite the brutal stinging of the water droplets, Gabe crept closer to the waterfall, finding a niche for his fingers here, a lump of clear rock there. Finally, he was just to the left of the cataract and beneath the chandelier. The bite of the spray kept him awake, at least, as he brought his trembling left arm around, toward the water. He let it wash over his glove and, reaching up, grabbed an icicle in his wet fist.

His glove froze fast.

He put his right glove in the water, reached up, and it too stuck to the ice. He looked up at the rounded mass that stretched some four feet to the top of the Face.

This was it, and the irony of everything once again hanging by a glove did not escape him. He began to pull himself up, trying to dig his boots or knee into the serac, intending to boost himself over the lip and scoot up before he slid off.

His biceps and pectoral muscles felt as if they were being branded: they burned, overloaded, and wanted to crash. Then they demanded it. Without having been able to get a toehold, Gabe eased back down.

His feet settled on two small rocks.

They gave.

With an oath, Gabe tensed his arms; one glove held, but the left one tore loose from the ice. Unable to reach the water, and with nothing to grab, he kicked ahead to find some support in the darkness under the ice cap. His boots smashed into huge icicles, which cracked and fell, leaving nothing at all in front of him.

Swinging wildly, he went limp, his three free limbs hanging straight down, lest he tear the glove, his lifeline, from the ice.

He was flagging quickly. Reaching up with his left hand, he locked his fingers between the fingers of the frozen glove. When he was sure he had a solid grip, he lifted his legs to the left, straight out, his abdominal muscles screaming as he brought his legs level with the lip of ice.

He was now horizontal and slightly higher than before, and could see a knob of ice a foot ahead. Praying his glove held, he pulled himself closer to it, rolling over his hands; when he was sure he could reach it, his left hand shot out, grabbed the ice, and pulled. He got his right knee up, then under him, then his boot, and then he pulled the other leg in. Still holding onto the sloping ice, squatting like a runner on the starting block, he made sure his crampons were dug in securely, then reached for a higher bulge on the ice, near the top. When he had it, he worked his hand from his glove, then scrambled up the rest of the serac.

He fell face-forward when he reached the top, his body shaking, his brain unsure whether to laugh or cry. He did a little of both, then forced himself to get up: he knew that if he lay there, the nap would be permanent.

THIRTY-TWO

The small, windowless little shack sat by the mouth of the mine shaft.

Years before, when she had first visited the place, Jessie had felt a rush of admiration for the man who'd built it, Gordon Douglas.

The yellowing photos on the wall told the tale. It was 1933. Douglas works a small mine here, and for relaxation does the first thorough geological survey of the area. His tools? Not light, alloy-metal pitons, but crude iron ones. Small, misaligned binoculars. A hard miner's hat. A heavy axe. He made climbs that were amazing by any yardstick, though the more so because of the crudeness of his tools.

Now, the Douglas Mine Shaft and Shack were a point of interest for tourists, with faux-antique lamps for lights and dusty old display cases filled with relics, ore, rock samples, diaries, clothing and other mementos. But to the rangers, it was something more than just a memorial or a photo opportunity. It was a testimonial to all climbers, mute evidence that mountains could be conquered if you had the skill and, just as important, the will.

Jessie brushed the snow from her clothing and was about

to light one of the lanterns when she heard footsteps outside. She turned and cracked the door, saw a figure shambling toward her.

"Gabe?"

She threw open the door.

"Gabe!"

The figure stopped a few feet away. "Jessie?" He hurried toward her. "Jess, what the hell are you doing here?"

"Looking for Hal. Frank dropped me in the west valley and I hiked."

She lit the lantern as Gabe entered and shut the door. She looked at him, squinting as her eyes adjusted to the light.

"My God—Gabe!" She reached out and touched his raw cheek. "Where's your coat? You're frozen."

"I'm all right."

"No you're not. Wait a second."

She turned to the wall, removed a pickax that was hanging there, and smashed one of the cases. She removed a motheaten sweater, shook off the particles of glass, and handed it to Gabe.

"That's better than nothing," she said.

Gabe slipped it on. "Thanks. But now you've gotta get out of here. You've gotta go back now."

"Why? Where's Hal? What's going on?"

He blew on his hands. "The distress call was a fake."

"I knew something was wrong—"

"It's a downed plane full of thieves. Before it crashed, they dumped or lost three cases of money. They've got Hal and are usin' him for a bird dog. Once they find the money, he's dead."

"Gabe, no. What can we do?"

"*We* aren't going to do anything. Get on your radio and contact Frank. Have him pick you up now, then contact the state police."

Jessie nodded and slipped the radio from its strap. She switched it on; nothing happened. She turned it off and on again. There was still just dead, thick silence.

"Looks like the cold's killed the batteries."

"Aw, shit," Gabe said.

"It's okay. Frank'll try to raise me, and when he can't he'll come looking for me. I told him I might come to the shack. When he gets here, we'll radio the police from the chopper."

"That's no good," Gabe said. "In two hours it's nightfall. There's no other shelter for ten miles, so Hal's likely to make for here. If they show, they'll take you."

"So what do you want me to do?"

"You've got no choice. Help me grab everything we can use and let's get the hell out of here. I think I know where the next case is located."

110

THIRTY-THREE

An early evening enveloped Qualen's group as the sun slid behind a tall peak. The sudden darkness, in addition to the snow and wind, made the going slow. The patches of ice beneath their feet were difficult to see, and there was harsh grumbling directed at Hal.

Not that he gave a damn. He couldn't think of anything but how he'd blamed Gabe all these months.

Grief was part of that, but guilt was also in the stew. Gabe hadn't let him down. He was just a man, a human being, a dude like him, doing the best job he could with the flesh and blood he'd been given. The truth was, Gabe had done the right thing. And he'd come close to working a miracle on that lifeline with Sarah, closer than Hal would've come on his best day.

The truth was, he was finally admitting to himself, he blamed Gabe because he didn't want to place the blame where it really belonged: on himself. He was the asshole who'd brought her up there. Gabe, who nearly died trying to fix his fuckup, was just a big, handy whipping boy. One who'd taken Hal's shit, lived with his own guilt, and still come back to help him today—dying trying to save him,

111

dying when he could have run.

God, how he regretted what he'd done to the guy.

Travers's raspy voice pulled him from his reverie.

"It's close," he said, looking up from the monitor. "Just up there."

"Better be," Kynette said, "or I'm gonna warm my toes up your ass."

"It's there all right, punk—and I'm getting real sick of your threats."

"Are you? Wanna do something about it?"

"I do," Qualen said. "I'd like to get Travers a brain and you a heart. But until we find the black metal boxes, the yellow brick road has to wait. Travers? Would you share the target with the rest of the class?"

With a snort of anger, the agent pulled off a glove with his teeth, pressed a button on the monitor, and lit the tracer light on the box.

Hal saw a dull, red glow wink on a quarter mile up the cliff. Half an hour to that box; if they didn't rest, maybe two hours to the next.

Maybe he'd just seen his last sunset, but he promised himself that when the time came, some way, somehow, he'd take Qualen with him. . . .

THIRTY-FOUR

Gabe and Jessie were hiking west and making good time, Gabe having gotten his second wind thanks to Gordon's gear and his way-musty but very warm sweater. Walking a few yards in front of Jessie, he saw the light before she did: it was too dim for a flare, and judging from its location, he knew what it had to be—a light on the box, just like the busted tracer he'd seen on the first one.

He stopped and pointed. "There it is. C'mon."

Though the sun had nearly set, they kept up their power-walking pace: he knew the mountain path, and he knew he had to get to the spot before Qualen did. The way Hal had to have taken them would get them here just after sunset, about a half hour from now . . . maybe a little longer if Hal managed to slow them down somehow. Not much of a window in either case.

Despite their haste, Gabe removed Gordon's hat and listened carefully as they hurried up the slope, hoping to avert a 9mm welcome if Qualen were already in the neighborhood.

They found the case amongst the trees. It was half buried beneath several inches of fresh snow, which Gabe and Jessie brushed away. Gabe removed the case.

"How much is in there?" Jessie asked.

"Thirty-three million in T-bills, give or take a grand."

She shook her head slowly. "And there are three of them?"

"Two now, after that deposit I made off Comb Bluff."

"You could buy a lot of hay with this."

"Or a lot of misery," he said, handing her the case. He hooked the end of his pick in the lock and pried it off. "Let's see if we can stir up some of our own."

THIRTY-FIVE

"This way," Travers said, Kynette's flashlight probing the ground before him as the hikers made their way around the base of a peak and up a rise. The agent was in the lead, Kynette was behind him, Delmar was next, Hal was in the middle, and Ryan, Kristel, and Qualen brought up the rear.

Hal stopped to kick and let Ryan pass him; he wanted to be close to Qualen in case there was any opportunity to knock him off a cliff, into a crevasse, against a tree, over a log, or just on his ass. It was funny, he thought, the things that suddenly seemed important when you had nothing else.

"It's just over this ridge," Travers said, pointing with the monitor.

"Then go—get it," Qualen said.

Travers didn't need to be told twice. He left the party, Kynette and Ryan following close behind, ducking low-lying branches and outrunning the reach of Qualen's flashlight.

Hal glanced back at Qualen. He looked and sounded tired. The man was obviously in good shape, but the air was thin, the climate was raw, and mountain climbing used leg and butt muscles that even someone who exercised diligently wouldn't have worked much. Sometime soon his guard would come down a little, and Hal would be there.

"Here!" Travers called from the top of the ridge. "Bring the light. It's over here among the trees!"

Qualen perked up and pushed Hal ahead. They hurried up the rise and lined up beside Travers and Kynette. Qualen swung his own light into the small clearing.

Qualen swore. Travers stared, dumbfounded, into the pit. Hal smiled.

Gabe was alive. He was alive, and he'd left them a snowman about three feet tall with a five-pebble smile and wearing what Hal recognized as Gordon Douglas's hat. The case was sitting at its roly-poly feet, but best of all was the nose: it was red and glowing.

The tracer.

Travers reached the snowman and dropped to his knees, flipped open the box. He reached in and pulled something out.

Qualen shined his flashlight on him. "What is it?"

"A thousand dollar bill," said Travers.

"Nothing else?"

Travers rose. "No." He kicked the snowman. "But there's something written on it."

"What?"

"It says, 'Wanna trade?' "

Hal watched Qualen, who was remarkably calm.

Travers crumpled the bill in his fist and punched the top of the snowman's head. The hat flew off, but the smile remained. "It's Walker! The son of a bitch's gotta be alive!"

Qualen looked at Ryan and Kynette. "You've got to respect a survivor. Mr. Tucker, you said there was no other way up here—"

"Except the East Face."

"Which you said was virtually impassable."

"Except for a psycho." Hal shrugged. "Guess the boy's got a new nickname." He'd never been prouder of anyone, ever. Qualen could shoot him now and he'd die a happy man.

But Qualen obviously wasn't thinking about killing him. The leader said to his henchmen, "He can't be far. There have to be footprints—find him. Go!"

Kristel took out a gun, put it to Hal's back, and pushed him to the east. Travers joined him, and the others moved out from the peak, north, west, and south, Ryan pausing to don nightvision goggles.

Five hundred feet above and just to the west, Gabe watched as the party fanned out in the wrong directions.

THIRTY–SIX

Ryan did a slow, careful three-sixty as he walked, peering into the darkness.

The others were looking at the ground, searching for prints; Kynette shouted that he'd found some.

Big fucking deal.

This Gabe dickhead would have expected them to find the prints and would have doubled back somewhere else. Or quickly moved somewhere he wouldn't leave prints.

Like rocks. The jerkoff was a ranger . . . a climber. He'd want to know what their next move was. He'd climb a cliff somewhere and watch. And the only cliff was to the east, where the mountain continued up who-the-fuck knew how high.

But shmucko wouldn't be too high up. He'd have gone a little way, sat down, and had a nice, long look-see.

So while Ryan turned around, pretending to head north, he was actually looking up with the nightvision goggles, the thousand-fold magnification of the crescent moonglow and starlight turning dark night into day. And lo and behold, in between the trees, down in a dip, was the twenty-nine

118

million, nine hundred and ninety-nine thousand dollar man himself with a companion—a woman!

Ryan smiled wickedly and continued to the north until he was out of view of the ledge where Walker was perched. Then, cutting back to the east, he began to move through the trees.

THIRTY-SEVEN

THIRTY-SEVEN

"How are you holding up?" Gabe asked Jessie.

"You know me. I'm a night person."

Gabe was staring through Douglas's old binoculars.

"How's Hal?"

"He's walking. Doesn't look like they've hurt him much. Right now, they're out searching for us. Guess they don't want to cut a deal. They've got to find shelter soon and so do we." He stood, wincing as he pulled on the backpack stuffed with money.

"What's wrong?"

"Been a long day," he said, "and I'm not as young as I used to be—"

Tree bark exploded where Gabe's head had been an instant before. He pulled Jessie down, landing on top of her as bullets raked the air above them.

When the shooting stopped, he pushed Jessie ahead, behind a boulder, and jumped after her.

They crouched there, listening.

"We're gonna have to run for it," Gabe whispered.

"Where?"

He looked west, through a wooded area. "You see that

clearing? Run for it. The trees'll give us some cover."

"And after that?"

"I don't know. We'll have to improvise. Go on three, and look out for the creek."

He counted it out, and they bolted from behind the rock, hunched over as they ran through the night.

Bullets alternately cut at the snow and the water, inches from their feet, giving Gabe strength and speed he didn't know he had. Jessie had it too, as they desperately ducked and dodged trees in the dark. After a few seconds, the bullets started falling short, then stopped. They were probably out of range or blocked by trees; in any case, whoever the bastard was, he or she was going to have to come after them.

He turned his head to the side, straining to hear over his crunching boots and hard breathing. He heard tree branches crack in the distance. They had a couple hundred yards on the shooter.

They cleared the woods, Jessie stopping so quickly that she lost her balance and fell on her side; Gabe dove for her, grabbing Jessie with one hand and a tree with the other. His quick action was all that kept them both from shooting down a sloping field of sheer ice. They'd reached the west face of the peak, the mouth of the creek.

Gabe saw a big rock on the other side of the ice.

"This way," he said, putting himself between her and the would-be killer as they made for it.

As they slid behind the rock, Gabe listened again.

The killer was coming—fast. Very fast. *Too* fast. And Gabe guessed why.

"You have flares in your pack?"

"Yeah—"

"Give me one."

Jessie fumbled in the dark and pulled one out. She handed it to him.

"I want you to double back wide and quiet and meet me at Eagle Cave."

"What about you?"

"Don't worry!" Gabe said urgently. "Just be ready to go when I tell you!"

The footsteps neared. He waited.

The *crunch, crunch, crunch* of boots on snow came nearer, then slowed, then stopped nearby. They'd seen the ice field, knew Gabe had to be around here somewhere. They were standing still, giving the place a once-over.

Not yet. He had to wait until he knew the person was coming toward him.

Crunch.

Gabe tensed.

Crunch. They'd figured it out or seen the footprints, were coming closer. Gabe waited until they took a few more steps, and Ryan clambered onto the boulder, then he ignited the flare and quickly stretched out, giving it a stiff-armed lob over the boulder.

He heard an agonizing scream.

"Go!" he said.

Jessie took off and Gabe leapt the boulder, hoping that the nightvision goggles had amplified the flare and left their pursuer blind.

They had. The man was about thirty feet away, and even in the dark Gabe could see that he was doubled over.

Doubled over, but not out of it. As Gabe approached, the man ripped off the goggles, threw them aside, and raised his gun. As Ryan's automatic spit bullets in a chest-high semicircle, Gabe threw himself forward, knocking the gun from Ryan's grasp. Gabe, Ryan, and the gun fell onto the ice field, sliding several feet apart.

Gabe scrambled to his feet. He looked for the gun, failed to find it, and lost precious seconds, time Ryan used to reach for the small ice axe hooked to his pack.

Gabe charged, tackling Ryan before he could get the gun. The two men spun forward again, locked together, their struggle causing them to skid farther down the ice, unable to stand or stop, skidding with increasing momentum toward the edge.

Fresher than his foe, Ryan was able to flip Gabe off and onto his back.

"You fuck!" Ryan screamed, sitting on his chest as they spun toward the edge. Ryan locked his hands and punched Gabe hard in the left temple. "You fucking *fuck*!"

Gabe took the blow. Ryan gave him another, on the right, and he took that too. And a third. The lumpy ice punched his spine painfully, but Gabe refused to let any of that distract him. Ryan was still too blind to realize that they were only about one hundred yards from a drop that would kill them both, and that there was only one way to stop from going over.

Having gathered his strength, Gabe heaved himself over on top of Ryan. Punching him, Gabe pushed his face into the frozen snow, ruts ripping away the flesh from one side.

As they continued to slide, Gabe reached out with his right hand and grabbed the axe. Ryan felt it slip from the leather loop.

"What the fuck—"

He realized too late what was happening. Gabe slammed it into the ice and stopped with a jerk; Ryan flew off his chest. Twisting frantically as he hit the ice, he grabbed the toe of Gabe's right boot. Gabe drove the spikes of his left boot into Ryan's hands and ground down hard. The man screamed, let go with one hand, then the other, then clawed at the ice as he struggled vainly to get a handhold. He was still screaming as he flew off the peak.

Gabe hung there over the ledge, held only by the axe, not thinking of anything but how much he hurt, from his calves to his forehead, inside and out, front to back.

Making sure the axe was secure, he edged to the right and looked over the side of the ice. There was a ledge underneath, about ten feet below and ten inches wide. Not a lot of room, but enough. Digging his boots into the ice, he pushed off and landed on the ledge, then vanished into the darkness.

THIRTY-EIGHT

Qualen's expression looked the same as it had when he saw the snowman, an odd blend of anger and amusement. He was like a pushmi-pullyu: Hal had never seen anything like it in his life.

This time, though, it wasn't a snowman Qualen's flashlight illuminated. It was a field of ice with a short smear of crystalline blood leading to a drop of nearly a mile. And a hole where someone had buried an axe. He could see it all, quite clearly, through the nightvision goggles Ryan had dropped.

Only Hal knew it was possible that Gabe had found a ledge beneath and climbed away to safety.

The guy wasn't just amazing, he was Rambo on ice.

Now Kristel held her Uzi and the discarded flare, and Qualen stood there with Ryan's nightvision goggles in one hand, the flashlight in the other, probably not thinking about the money but about the fact that there was someone better at the survival game than him. It was his ego that was hurting, not his Swiss bank account.

Qualen took a few steps closer to the blood. He sighed.

"Yeah," Hal said. "Gravity's a bitch."

Kristel was thinking about the money. Roaring with rage, she knocked him down with the butt of her Uzi.

"If you think gravity's a bitch, you don't know me!" She turned to Qualen. "Are we going after him?"

"No."

"But he went back into the woods—we can catch him."

"He knows this mountain; we don't."

"He also knows where the third box is!"

"Yes, he does," Qualen said. "But even if he finds it, he'll be reasonable."

"Reasonable?!" Delmar sneered. "This guy threw Ryan off a fucking cliff!" He turned and started walking away. "That's it! Fuck the money and fuck it all."

Kynette shouted, "Losin' your nerve, Brit?"

Delmar stopped and took a few steps back. "You sayin' somethin' to me, boy?"

"Yeah. I'm sayin' you're a wimp to get spooked by some mountain geek."

"You think *Ryan* was a wimp?"

Qualen stepped between them. "Enough! The fight's not here—not anymore. It's out there!"

"Maybe bigger'n you think," Delmar said. "How do we know this Walker turd hasn't gone for help?"

"Because I wouldn't."

Delmar's face screwed up in confusion.

"A tracker who strays far from his quarry," said Qualen, "even a good tracker, runs the risk of losing the spoor. And he won't risk losing ours. Not while we have something he wants." He pointed the gun down at Hal. "Now, something—where's the nearest shelter?"

"You mean a cave?"

Qualen smiled. "That's shelter for an animal, Mr. Tucker. A bear, a fox, a rescue ranger. No. I mean a shelter for people."

"There's a shack about three miles from here."

"As the crow walks, without climbing?"

Hal nodded.

"Fine. Lead the way. We'll rest a bit and then see if we can't surprise Mr. Walker a little more effectively than our late, lamented ninja master was able to do."

At a command from Qualen, Delmar and Kynette walked over and lifted Hal to his feet, sneering at each other and him and the mountain as they headed off to the Douglas Mine Shaft and Shack.

Though Hal was tired, he knew he had to feel better than everyone else, and that kept him going. He took a short detour as they headed toward the shack, coming toward it over the mine: that way, he could dislodge rocks as they climbed down, alert Gabe in case he'd come here.

When they arrived, and the flashlight beams played across the busted door, Hal knew that Gabe had already been and left. The team followed him in, their lights shining on the broken display cases, the axe-shaped silhouette on the wall, the fresh-looking spots on the wood floor where ropes had been removed after decades.

"Rough weather they got up here," Kynette said.

Travers looked down into one of the empty cases. "No, Walker was here. What was in these, Tucker?"

"Nothing."

Delmar kneed him in the kidneys. "You're lyin'."

"Nuts to you! Just rocks were in there, relics of the mine."

Qualen had been standing in a corner. He stepped over, shining the light in Hal's face. "Why would Mr. Walker want rocks?" Qualen looked at the photographs on the walls. "I think he took equipment from the shack. Correct, Mr. Tucker?"

"There wasn't much here."

"Not much . . . but *something*. And he took it because, as I said, he doesn't plan on going anywhere. He plans on staying close to his friend."

"You've got it wrong, mister," Hal said. "He's not a friend of mine."

"Nice try. But I never underestimate the persistence of loyalty when it comes naturally," he glanced at Kynette, "as compared to having to pay for it."

Kynette shifted his bulk from foot to foot. "Hey, c'mon, Boss. That ain't fair."

Qualen faced Hal. "You see? I've companions *and* philosophers. I'm rich in so many ways." He pointed to Hal's backpack with his flashlight. "You brought matches?"

Hal nodded.

"Good. Make a fire. Delmar, Kynette—break up these cases and the rest of the door. We're going to stay for a while."

THIRTY-NINE

As the frigid winds howled against the green nylon of the portable tent, Brett warmed his hands over a small kerosene heater and scowled at his partner, who was gnawing on a rock-hard candy bar.

"Here's a notion," Brett said. "Next time you're like watching MTV, y'know, take a nanosecond or two and flip it to the weather channel and check out the broadcast for, y'know, major storms and catastrophes. I mean, hey, where would you rather be now: here in tent city, or home playin' air hockey?"

"Air hockey's got my vote."

"Exactly, cheesehead, exactly."

Evan looked hurt. "Cheesehead?"

Brett nodded and they fell silent.

"Y'know," Evan said around a mouthful of nougat and chocolate, "*you* were the homeboy who told Gabe that you liked your weather conditions extreme."

"Extreme, yes. Friggin' surface-of-Pluto cold and blowy, no."

Evan chewed for a moment, lost in thought. This storm was a real bitch, and they were unprepared.

Stupid, in these parts, and they knew it. This could be real trouble if it didn't let up.

"Gabe," he sighed. "He's probably back in Denver, watchin' a tape, contemplating something of the Julia Roberts gender—"

"Instead of freezing his ass off on a snowbound cliff. I ask you: who made out today, him or us?"

FORTY

Gabe and Jessie were sitting crosslegged, side by side, at the fire they'd built in Eagle Cave. His face was bruised and his fingertips were frostbitten, but he felt surprisingly hale; he was achy but pumped and mentally alert, thinking about Qualen and Hal and Frank. He was glad the weather had stayed lousy; Frank would be worried, but at least he couldn't have taken off. For the night, at least, Qualen was going to have to stay put.

The stacks of money were burning quickly, so Gabe reached over and threw another three in.

"That makes three million bucks in a half-hour," he said. "It costs a fortune to heat this place."

Jessie smiled, but without conviction.

"What's wrong?"

"Gabe, I'm so worried about Hal."

"Yeah, I've been thinking about him too. But he's tough. If I can keep them off-balance, he'll be okay."

Jessie squeezed his hand. "No matter what happens, you're not responsible for this. Don't put that on yourself."

He half smiled and stretched his legs. "You know, it's strange."

"What is?"

"These past months I've been telling myself all I want to do is live the rest of my life with no problems, keep one step ahead of them. But you're always responsible to someone or someplace or something, no matter what. I tried to leave this morning, Jess. I really did. But you can't run from yourself or what you are." He looked at her. "A woman I know once said that."

"Where is she now?"

"Real close," he said, touching her cheek. "You were right not to leave with me. I do belong here."

He moved toward her, she bent closer to him, and they kissed in the firelight. Gabe hadn't kissed her for nearly a year, but when their lips touched, he felt he'd never been away, knew how lucky he was that she was still here.

It was good to be one again.

He broke the kiss. "They're gonna find us frozen together if we're not careful."

"I don't mind."

"You will if we've gotta do any running." Gabe overturned his backpack and emptied a half dozen more stacks onto the fire. "Lay down and get some rest. We're gonna need it."

She scooted back a bit and lay on her side, Gabe next to her, facing her back.

"Gabe?"

"Yeah."

"If you're not using your arm, can I borrow it?"

"Sure," he said, slipping it under her and pulling her close.

FORTY-ONE

"Hal, Jessie . . . do you read? Again, do you read? Come in! What the hell's going on up there?"

Travers turned down the volume button on the radio. Qualen was standing in the doorway looking out at the sunrise. It was a briskly cold morning but clear.

"Jessie?" Qualen said to Hal. "Looks as if we're drawing a crowd. Why didn't he say anything about Mr. Walker?"

Hal hobbled over, aching from all the blows he'd taken the day before. "I told you—nobody likes the guy. He's a leper. Frank doesn't even know he's up here."

"What will this Frank do?"

"Stay on the radio till he gets an answer, probably."

"Why won't he send help?"

"There's no help to send. The state police don't like coming here."

"They don't like it, but will if they have to—"

"Just as spotters," Hal said. "They won't land."

Travers said, "So what you're telling us is, in a few hours the whole fucking world will show up here."

"What can I say? Your parties are a hot ticket."

Travers said, "Then we'd better get moving." He slipped the monitor from around his neck and shoved it in front of Hal. "Where's the next one?"

Hal looked at the monitor, then stepped to the door and pointed. "It's up there. On that peak."

"How far?" Qualen asked.

Hal's eyes dropped to the mine just fifty yards away. It had been too dark to go before, but now he toyed with making a break for it.

Travers ran over and grabbed Hal's hair. "He asked you how far?! And not the scenic route. How far from here to there?"

"Half a day!"

Travers released him. "Come on," he said to Qualen. "I don't want that other prick beating us to it again!"

"Point well taken," Qualen said. He pushed Hal out and followed him, then motioned to the others.

Rested and eager, the team started out briskly, making their way quickly through the wooded, gently sloping terrain at the foot of the Tower. Whenever Hal edged them closer to a precipice, Qualen would wave him back with the gun; he may have wanted to lose some of his teammates, but he didn't want to risk losing his guide.

And then Hal saw a sight that made his heart miss a beat.

"Hey, man!"

Two figures—Brett and Evan in their glasses—jumped up and waved at him from a small, sheltered area near the cliff.

"Hey, Hal!" said Brett. "Hey, man, you jammed up here too?"

Hal waved back but didn't head over.

"Who is it?" Qualen asked.

"Their names are Brett and Evan. Rich kids. You don't want to cross their families."

"Walk over."

"For Christ's sake, Qualen, they're *kids*."

"We're not animals, Mr. Tucker. Now walk over. And smile."

Doing as he was told, Hal headed stiffly toward the duo, Kynette following part of the distance.

"Hey, man!" Evan low-fived him as he neared. "Was that storm a severe bummer or what? We were in tent city last night."

"Yeah," Hal said dryly. "It was a bummer."

"We're gonna take one more jump and split," Brett said. He lifted his shades and looked around Hal. "So what's the dish? You baby-sitting lost hikers?"

"You got it."

"I see a babe—"

"She's taken, Brett."

Evan punched Hal in the arm, then finished buckling his backpack. "You stud, you!"

"Introduce us, man," Brett said, walking around him and heading for the group.

"Brett, don't! We're really pressed for time—"

"Word to your mother, Hal. Maybe they want to try a jump or split a candy bar."

"Yeah, chill out, Hal," Evan said and started walking away.

"Evan, no! Shit, man, run!"

Brett turned around but kept walking. "What?"

"I said *run*, goddammit!"

Hal ran after him, watching over his shoulder as Kynette slid his automatic from behind his back, held it waist-high, and opened fire. Brett was nearly cut in two by a burst of thirty rounds.

135

Hal kept running toward them. Evan stopped.

"You son of a bitch!" Hal roared. "You said you wouldn't kill him!"

"Sue us."

From the corner of his eye, Hal saw Evan break for the woods, Kynette and Travers in pursuit. Hal threw a shoulder against Qualen's chest, and the two men fell on the snow, Hal swinging a fist down and missing as Qualen ducked his head to the side.

Hal looked to his right just in time to catch the butt of Kristel's gun in his forehead. He fell back, his vision aswirl with red, ears ringing, bolts of pain flitting around his skull.

"Never touch him!" she snarled.

Delmar bent him in two with a kick in the stomach. "You're a dead man, asshole."

Hal peered through the clouds of red and saw Evan weaving through the trees, headed for the cliff, Kynette and Travers racing to get a shot at him.

"Go, man, go," Hal wheezed under his breath, hoping that if Evan made it to the edge, he'd have the presence of mind to break the first rule of jumping. . . .

FORTY-TWO

Gabe and Jessie were moving along the rock wall below the Tower. Though the mountainside was relatively sheer here, there were shelves that allowed them both handholds and places to rest Gabe's sore limbs. Unless Hal had started out before dawn, as they had—which Gabe very much doubted—and unless Qualen and his gang were going to climb the face of the Tower, as they were, Gabe knew he had a good shot at getting to the third box before them. The key was how long it took to take *his* route up the Tower.

They were taking a breather when they heard the gunfire.

"Hal!" Jessie said, her brow knitting with concern.

Gabe stepped back to the edge of the shelf, looked up at the cliff some four hundred feet above and a quarter mile to the south. He heard movement, footsteps coming closer, then saw a figure go flying off the edge, arms and legs splayed.

"Evan?" he said.

Jessie looked up. "It must be. That's his Sprockets jacket—only one like it. But where's Brett? They always jump together."

As the figure sailed down, two others appeared at the edge of the cliff. Gabe tensed as he recognized them, saw that one of them had a rifle. Jessie gasped.

"Gabe, they're armed. Are they part of—"

"Yeah," he said, "they're Qualen's apes." He continued to watch Evan. "Pull in your arms, man, and forget the ten count. Don't pull the cord till you're out of range."

Gabe looked up. Travers was trying to pull the rifle from Kynette.

"Shoot him!" Travers yelled, his voice echoing down the slope.

Kynette raised the rifle, fired, missed.

Evan pulled in his arms and feet. "Good man," Gabe said. He was already below them, having fallen nearly two thousand feet.

"Is he going to make it?" Jessie asked.

"Depends on how good a shot the guy is and how long Evan can keep his finger off the D-ring—"

Even as he spoke, the parachute billowed under them, tugging Evan up and rocking in the updraft.

"No!" Gabe looked up, saw Kynette aiming. "Too soon, man! Too damn soon!"

He looked up again, feeling nearly as helpless as he'd felt watching Sarah die.

Travers was yelling at Kynette, who was staring down the gun sight.

"Blast him! You're letting him get away!"

"Yeah? Let's see how good you are, agent man."

He handed Travers the rifle. The agent didn't waste a second: he threw it against his shoulder, aimed, and fired.

Gabe looked down as a bullet pierced the canopy. A splash of red erupted from the top of Evan's jacket.

"Oh, God," Jessie said.

Evan was still moving, tugging on the shroud lines, trying

to land on the other side of a high hill. He cleared the hill but caught a tree, the chute snagging on a low branch, Evan jerking to a stop and dangling limply below, a few feet from the ground. Except for the wind-rustled fabric, there was no further movement.

Shaking with rage, Gabe looked up and saw Qualen, Hal, and the others standing near the edge. The woman had a gun to Hal's temple. Gabe eased Jessie back toward the mountain and took a step back himself, though he could still see the gang, and hear what they were saying.

"Might catch on," Qualen said. "Like shooting skeet."

"Murdering motherfucker . . . " Hal hissed.

"There you are," Qualen said. "Kill a few people, they call you a murderer. Kill a few million, you're called a conqueror. Go figure." He pushed Hal around. "Now it's time to move on, Tucker. Time, like life, is short."

The gang moved away, and Gabe turned to Jessie. "Can you keep going?"

She nodded.

He continued along the ledge to the north, toward the Tower, wanting to do more than just beat the gang to the money. Somehow, he was going to turn the Tower into hell for that cocky bastard and his pirates. A hundred million dollars? That was just part of what they were going to pay for Evan's life.

The climb to the foot of the Tower was relatively easy, though as Gabe looked through Douglas's binoculars, across the tree-lined plain, he saw that Qualen wasn't taking any chances. The Tower was ahead. The cliff Evan had jumped from was behind. Qualen had formed two groups: he was up ahead with Hal, Travers, and the woman; his two remaining gorillas were several hundred feet behind. No one could come at either group from behind or from the front without the other group coming to their rescue.

Gabe scanned the area in front of them. Hal was leading them to a buttress, a large boulder formation that lay before the Tower. They'd have to go up on all fours, though the first group would be safely on top before the second one started up. Again, they'd be protected from any kind of sneak attack.

Jessie folded her arms against the wind, stood there shivering. "Anything?"

"Yeah. He's taking them the long way around. Qualen's probably figured that the only way anyone can get past him is by helicopter."

"But you know better, right?"

Gabe swung the ancient binoculars to the west, where a wall of brush crept up the side of the Tower.

"Put it this way, Jess. Y'know that trip I told you about, the one I took up the East Face yesterday?"

"Yes. . . ."

"That was a warm-up, a semifinal."

Gabe fished her hand from her folded arms and squeezed it. They started toward the west, her hand still in Gabe's, though her mind was obviously back on the cliff . . . on Evan.

Gabe hurt for the kid too, but he couldn't afford to think about him. He kept his eyes on Qualen's party. They'd cleared the buttress and were on their way up the peak, most of them on all fours, none of them bothering to look back. They hadn't seen anyone when they shot Evan, and figured that anyone coming from that direction would be way behind.

Hal, of course, would know differently. He'd also know he had to stall here and there to buy Gabe time. Gabe had grave doubts about what he was planning to do. Never mind

140

beating Qualen: just surviving would be a trick. Months before the accident with Sarah, he and Hal had come up to help a climber who said she'd been bitten by a wolverine. Since there weren't supposed to be any this far south, he and Hal had tracked it to the west, found the starving rogue, got it to eat, then had Jessie come and helicopter it to a lower altitude. Meanwhile, trying to figure out how it had gotten here, they found a crevice that ran straight through the Tower, from the top to the bottom, one that had to have been opened by a long-ago earthquake, a rift that was remote and overgrown with foliage and covered with snow and had never been marked on any map. A fissure that looked like a straight line drawn by Picasso.

A long, tight, killer crevice that they were going to have to climb. He certainly didn't want Jessie coming with him, though short of picking up a branch and knocking her out, he didn't see how he was going to get her to stay behind.

Gabe led the way when they reached the brush, pushing it aside and tamping it down for Jessie, trying to think of what he could say or do that would get her to take a rain check.

Reason, he finally decided. He would show her the crevice and try to reason with her.

When they cleared the brush, they stood before a shaft that disappeared into the ground below and into the peak above. The crack ranged from six inches to six feet across, and moved upward for a dozen or so yards, then off to the left, then straight up again, then parallel to the ground, then up again.

Gabe watched Jessie's eyes as they moved up the crevice.

"And this is just the outside," he said. "Hal and I once went in a little—it goes all the way through, to the Tower, but the geometry is all screwed up. You've got to go up, then down, just to go straight."

"What's the worst it gets?"

"We stopped at a long section where there's just roof and no floor. You have to go through upside down." He faced her, held her at arm's length. "Jess, I don't want anything to happen to you. Why don't you—"

"Stuff it, Gabe." She turned her back, walked to the crevice and stopped. "You coming, or do I go alone?"

Gabe looked over with resignation, then walked to the rift, took off his backpack, peered into the dark interior, and tried to figure out the best way to begin. . . .

FORTY-THREE

One thousand feet up, on the adjoining peak, Hal stood in front of Qualen's party as they joined him on the summit. They stood in a semicircle and looked toward the Tower. All of them were breathing heavily, and Travers's teeth were chattering—more from anticipation than from the cold, Hal suspected. Qualen didn't seem happy.

"You said there was a way across."

"There is."

Travers moved ahead several paces. He looked down. "Then where the fuck is it?"

"There." Hal pointed down.

Travers took several cautious steps forward, to where the peak sloped down again, sharply. The mountains were just fifteen feet apart right below: between them was a bridge made of rope and timber. The rope looked weatherbeaten and worn; several of the planks were broken and two were missing.

"This is insane!" Travers turned to Qualen. "The hell with the money! You radio in for that chopper and get us the hell out of here, you understand?"

"I do. You don't. We're in bed, Travers. Brothers in

crime. Joined at the hip. You crossed over and there's no crossing back."

Qualen looked down at the bridge. "Mr. Tucker—where is the case relative to our present position?"

"Over the bridge and about a quarter mile down the Tower."

"Why didn't we just climb the Tower?"

"Too steep. We can go back and try, if you want."

Qualen studied him. "Why do I get the feeling that you neglected to mention the bridge on purpose?"

"Because you're paranoid?"

Kristel shot him a menacing look.

"Yes, that must be it," Qualen said. He turned and drove the toe of his boot hard into Hal's groin. "For future reference, I don't like surprises. See that there are no more between here and the case."

Hal was on his knees, fighting for breath.

Kristel smiled down at him.

Hal planned to get her too.

Travers had gone down to get a closer look at the bridge. "Qualen, if I *spit* on this thing, it's coming down!"

"Think of it as a theme park attraction," Qualen said. "That will make it more palatable." He grabbed Hal's shoulder and pulled him up. "I will be crossing last, Mr. Tucker. If the bridge *should* collapse at any point, either Kristel or I will kill you, and then your friends at the ranger station."

"You'll do that anyway," he moaned.

"Perhaps. But money puts me in a good mood, and I may decide to be lenient. It will be worth your while to see if that happens. Get it? Got it?"

He nodded once.

"Good. Kristel—ladies first."

FORTY-FOUR

During his years as a ranger, Gabe had been in a cave-in at the mine, he'd been stuck in a pit when the dirt wall collapsed, and he'd even stumbled into a pool of quicksand. But this was the closest he'd ever come to feeling like he was buried alive.

They had been able to shimmy straight up the first dozen yards, then left, and were now going up again. Simultaneously, they worked their way sideways, to avoid a foot-wide section directly above.

But the eighteen-inch section they were in wasn't much better. The rock was cold, the air was moldy, there was a rotten smell they couldn't quite place, and their backpacks—which they were dragging beside them—were getting heavy.

Gabe stopped. Jessie was to his right, breathing heavily, fitting a little easier than he was but not enjoying it any more. They didn't need to rest on anything: just pointing their toes forward provided all the pressure they needed to stand.

He raised Jessie's flashlight with his left hand, shining

it up and to the side to see if there was more room to the west.

"Well?" Jessie asked.

"Don't move."

"Why?"

"I found out what's causing the smell I've been smelling."

He moved his head slightly to the left so she could see over it: what she saw were bats. Scores of them hanging on the wall to the left and above them.

Jessie put her face down and started to gag. "I'm going down and then under them," she said and began inching down.

"Jess, no! Don't move! Their hearing's for shit, but they'll feel—"

His words were drowned out by the sudden explosion of screeches and the distinctive, leathery flap of wings. The duo wasn't a target, but they were in the way as the bats moved out, seeking to get deeper into the crevice, away from the light, farther from the intruders.

Jessie screamed as they fluttered around her, brushing her with their warm bellies and cold wings, their sharp toes and wing-thumbs raking her face and hair. Most of them were still wet with dew, which shook loose on her as they passed.

"It's all right," Gabe was saying as they flew past. "Jess—your voice is gonna carry! They may hear us outside!"

She stopped screaming, but even after the wave had gone by and only a few stragglers remained, she continued to tremble.

Gabe put his hand on her head, and she jumped.

"It's only me," he said.

She was shaking. He held her arm, in case she let go with her feet and slipped down, and tried to soothe her. After a

146

minute, she said she was all right.

"Actually," Gabe told her, "you did a good thing."

"Wh-what do you mean?"

He shone the flashlight ahead. "We can go that way. Coast's clear now."

She took a steadying breath, then followed him on a diagonal course ahead.

FORTY-FIVE

Though his eyes stung and his senses were on the slow side from a night of no sleep, Frank had taken off in the chopper at first light, and headed to where he'd left Jessie the day before.

He waited a half hour, and when she didn't show, he took off again, flying low and fast over the treetops and snow, headed toward the Douglas Mine, one eye on the infrared screen mounted to the dash. If she were anywhere within a square mile below, he'd find her.

A buzzer sounded; there was a blip on the screen. To the north, in an area near the base of the Tower. Putting the Huey into a tight roll, he soared toward the clearing, his eyes on the ground, the radio turned way up to make sure even his sleep-deprived ears could hear her.

But it wasn't Jessie he spotted.

A body was hanging below a parachute, a trio of wolves circling below it, one of them hopping up, falling just short of the figure's heel. The animals stopped and looked up as the chopper circled the figure, but they didn't flee; food was scarce in the winter.

Having landed the chopper several dozen yards away, Frank took a pistol from a bracket on the wall, stepped out, and fired several shots into the air. All but the leaping wolf fled. Frank came closer, fired lower. The last animal ran off and Frank ran forward.

As he neared, he heard the boy moan. When he reached the tree, he pulled a folding knife from his belt and laid the gun on the ground. With his shoulder against the boy's waist, he reached up and cut away the shroud lines, catching him as he fell. Only then did he see the wound.

Evan moaned again.

"Hey, you've been shot!" Frank said. "Hang on—you're gonna be fine. I'll have you to a hospital in no time."

Breathless, straining under the weight of the boy, he ran back to the chopper, laid him gently on the ground, then opened the door and pulled out the cot. He attached the cradle to the skid, laid the boy on it, covered him with a blanket, and was quickly airborne. After calling the hospital in town and telling them to have paramedics waiting for him at the station, he prayed that the poor kid lived—and that Jessie hadn't needed him.

FORTY-SIX

It took time for Gabe and Jessie to work out their rhythm, but when they got it they made good time. Gabe would leave his backpack with her, climb a few feet, reach down for the pack and her hand, help her up, then repeat. The crack was accommodating enough to give them the room to maneuver without having to use their equipment . . . or detour for bats.

But their luck changed as they reached a section that, for as far as they could see in either direction, was no wider than a mail slot.

"What now?" Jessie asked.

"Stay where you are. I'll go to the side to see if there's a way up there."

"Be careful," she said.

Gabe sidled to the left, his head facing in the same direction in case there wasn't room to turn it up ahead.

"Looks good," he said, peering into a passage that went up diagonally in the direction they'd just come, forming the stem of a giant L and rising at least as far as the end of the flashlight beam. He twisted so he could look up the passage, his right forearm and knees against the wall in front, trying to see if it was wide enough to rig ropes. The tunnel had a slight curve at the bottom that made it difficult to see; he edged his legs to the left so his torso was pointing right and he could poke his head and the flashlight up.

He got them partway up, but needed to shift his legs a little farther to the left—

The wall behind his backside sloped away suddenly and he slid down. Gabe tried to grab the wall in front of him, but there was nothing to hold onto and he continued to slide down and left as the crack widened. The flashlight *clink-clanked* against the wall as he tried to brace himself in the widening passageway.

"Gabe?! *Gabe!*"

He clutched the flashlight as his jacket caught, tore, caught and tore again as he pinballed downward, hitting the wall in front, the wall behind, unable to stop himself. He was on his side then, facing downward, the beam of the light showing the end of the passageway a few yards below, and below that—nothing.

Quickly pulling himself into a ball, he pressed his spine against one wall, let the light go, locked his fists, and pushed both forearms and both knees against the other wall. He scraped to a halt inches from the end, hanging upside down like a bat, watching the light tumble end over end as it was swallowed up in the blackness.

FORTY-SEVEN

Qualen sent Hal across the bridge after Kristel, guns trained on the ranger from both sides. But Hal wasn't what was on Qualen's mind as he crossed. He could have sworn he heard voices—one of them familiar—coming from somewhere below.

He motioned Kynette over.

"When you cross, we'll go ahead, but I want you to stay behind."

"What's up?"

"The other ranger may be around here somewhere."

"I thought I heard something. I figured it was other outdoors assholes." Kynette looked across at the Tower. "I'll go to a higher point and keep a lookout—flank him if he shows."

"Good. One thing, though."

"Huh?"

Qualen walked toward the bridge. "Don't kill him until you get the money."

FORTY-EIGHT

"Gabe, what happened?!"

He was breathing heavily from fear and stress, but at least he didn't have to work to stay put. His coiled body was doing that for him.

"I fell."

"Are you all right? What should I do?"

"Can you get to the rope in my backpack?"

He heard her moving and grunting. "Yeah."

"Okay. Throw it down one end and go left *slowly*."

Jessie did as he instructed, and when the rope brushed against his cheek, Gabe leaned into his right forearm to brace himself, then carefully reached his left hand out and grabbed the rope.

"What's it attached to?" he asked.

"My waist," Jessie said. "It's okay. I'm secure."

Holding tight with his left hand, Gabe swung his right to the line and climbed, reaching Jessie in just a few long pulls. He looked at her in the flickering glow of her lighter.

"It seemed a lot longer when I was falling." He smiled. "Glad you came."

"Thanks. Does this mean we're going to be late?"

"It's possible," Gabe said, starting back toward the right. "But Hal should be okay. Even if they get the case, they'll still need a ranger to get out of here."

The two shimmied up the passageway, backs to one wall, arms stiff against the other, until the tunnel leveled off sufficiently so they could ascend on all fours. But the respite was short-lived. The passageway ended here in a vertical tunnel nearly a yard in diameter. The tunnel was dark on top, probably ending without an outlet. They could hear water running and hear it trickling down the rocks around them.

But mist glinted faintly in the air around them; light had to be coming from somewhere. Gabe had Jessie hold his belt so he could lean back and look up the wall on their side.

"Bingo!" he said.

Jessie was grunting, leaning back as a counterbalance. "What is it?"

"Six or seven feet up—our passage doubles back and continues up diagonally."

"Can we use the pitons?"

He motioned for her to pull him in. "Not enough room to swing the hammer. I'll have to jump it."

"Seven *feet*?"

"I'll be okay," he said, tying the rope around his waist and leaving her with the backpacks.

His plan was simple: a carom shot, using himself as the billiard ball. He stood at the end of the passageway, facing the opposite wall, and lit the lighter again. There were outcroppings of rock everywhere, none of them big enough to hold onto for long, but some of them large enough to buy him a second or two on the wall. With just a little luck and the help of his crampons—

He saw the rocks he wanted, about three feet up. Bending at the knees, he threw back his arms and jumped. He got to the rocks, slammed in his spikes, and quickly turned so his face was toward his goal, the passageway on the right. He coiled his legs, and with his crampons holding him in place for the second he needed, he simultaneously twisted his torso, stretched his arms, and sprung toward the ledge. He flew right in, landing flat and with a thud, then immediately started backsliding. He dug in his fingers and toes, dragged loose dirt down with him, scratched desperately at the walls of the tunnel, and managed to get a handhold on both sides.

He looked ahead. There *was* light and he saw that it was good.

Gabe yelled for Jessie to be ready to come up, then used the ice axe to carve handholds and make his way to the top.

Gabe broke through the snow on top with the ice axe.

The air was cold but tasted delicious when he finally poked his head through the crack in the boulder-covered summit of the Tower. After getting his bearings and spotting the rope bridge Qualen would have to cross to reach here, he squeezed out. Wrapping one end of the rope around a rock, he lowered the other end into the rift.

"Come on! I'll pull you up!"

"Do you see them?" Jessie called back as she moved into position.

"No," Gabe said. He took off his gloves for a better grip on the rope. "But we're on the right side of the bridge. With any luck, we can cut it down before they get to it."

Gabe heard a click and turned.

"Walker," Kynette said, standing behind a boulder, his machine gun tucked under his arm. "Sorry to have to say it, but this *ain't* your lucky day."

FORTY-NINE

The sleek, silver, four-seat Aero Spatiale AS 350 B.I. chopper sliced through the Rockies, its rotor gleaming in the sunlight, its undercarriage hopping along the morning thermals. Inside, Federal Aviation Agent Julianne LaFond was at the controls. Head Comptroller Wright was seated next to her, and Deputy Comptroller Davis and Agent Stewart were in the seats behind her. After frustrating storm-related delays, they were finally searching for the Treasury jet, hoping it hadn't strayed from its flight path and that if it had gone down, they might spot the wreckage and any survivors.

"Communication for you!" LaFond shouted, pointing to his headphone-mouthpiece unit.

Wright nodded, pressed his own headphone to his ear, and adjusted the mike. He hated flying, and earphones always made him nauseated. It was an association thing going back to the first time he flew. His older brother had rented him a headset and he was listening to the pop channel, with its Helen Reddy selection, when the plane took off and he puked. Since then, whenever he flew, put on headphones, or heard "I Am Woman," he felt ill. A combination of all three was deadly.

He swallowed hard. "Wright here."

"Mr. Wright, FBI Agent Michaels. The FAA satellite has found your jet. Our men are heading over to look for survivors."

"How's it look?" Wright said.

"Its wreckage is scattered over a two-mile area, miles off course. We're not hopeful for survivors."

"I see."

"We've also ID'd your dead pilot. He flew for Qualen when the guy was still legit."

"And Qualen made him an offer he couldn't refuse."

"Something like that. What we'd like you to do, though, is swing around and take a look at another aircraft we've pinpointed. Is the pilot on?"

"I'm here," she said.

"Fly one hundred and ten miles south of your present location." He gave her the exact coordinates, then said, "You're looking for a Jet Star—from the looks of it, the wings are gone and it's cracked in half. Reconnoiter, but do not land. Repeat: do *not* land."

"Copy."

"Agent Michaels," Wright said, "what's the big whoop about the jet?"

"It belongs to Qualen. If he was trying to make off with your money, it doesn't look like he made it."

Wright put the headphones down and squeezed the arm-rests as LaFond turned the chopper practically on its side and shot southwest. He closed his eyes, looking forward to mixing it up with an international terrorist instead of a pilot who had obviously grown up listening to the same song he had. . . .

FIFTY

Gabe wedged himself at the top of the hole. Kynette came around the boulder, the machine gun trained in Gabe's direction.

"Who's down there?" Kynette asked.

"Nobody. I'm alone."

"Want me to fire down the rabbit hole, *ass*hole?"

Gabe shook his head. "It's another ranger."

"The lady ranger?"

Gabe nodded.

"Okay, hotshot. Ya wanna buy some life? Where's the money?"

"Gone."

"What the fuck you talking about? Where is it?"

"I burned it. Never could save a thing."

Kynette stepped closer, but not close enough for Gabe to reach. The gun was steady. So was Kynette's gaze. The guy might have had the IQ of toast, but he knew how to be a heavy.

"Listen, Mr. Funny Fucking Man," Kynette said. "I never make deals, but with you I'll make one. Give over the money and I'll kill just you, not the girl. Because I'm a gentleman, her I'll just—"

"Gabe?"

Kynette's eyes shifted to the hole when Jessie shouted; Gabe knew what he had to do.

He waited until Kynette was right there, then pulled the axe from the snow and swung hard. The blade slashed through the heavy cloth and tore a hunk of flesh from Kynette's leg.

Kynette fired as he went down, the bullets ricocheting off the rocks. But Gabe was already gone. He'd grabbed the rope and screamed as he fell through the narrow passageway back down into the cave.

"Gabe!" Jessie cried.

He winced as gunshots sounded in the tunnel, echoing loudly, bullets pinging as they continued to bounce around him. He bumped into Jessie, who had stopped where the rope did, near the end of the passageway.

Gabe stayed on top of Jessie, shielding her, as Kynette continued to fire; when the shooting stopped, he flopped onto his back and pressed his hands to the cool rock wall above.

Jessie's face was barely visible in the dark. She took one of his hands, looked at it, then slipped off her backpack and got the first aid kit.

"Still glad I came back?" Gabe asked as he pulled her back through the passageway.

"Sure," she said.

FIFTY-ONE

Qualen's radio beeped, and he signaled ahead for Kristel to stop. With a smile of anticipation, he slipped the unit from its belt strap.

"Kynette, have you seen him?"

"Yeah, Boss."

"What's going on? Where's the money?"

"Not here. He, uh—he said he torched it."

Qualen's eyes darkened. "He's a joker. He was kidding."

"I don't think so."

The smile was gone. "Where is he now?"

"Gone. He dropped down into a cave."

"He what?!"

"I couldn't do anything, man. He knows this place like he knows his own goddamn bathroom!"

Qualen was squeezing the radio as though it were Kynette's neck. "Where are you?"

"At a crack on top of the mountain, about thirty yards higher an' north of the bridge."

"Fine. You had your chance. Move it out now!"

"Forget it. I'm takin' him out."

"I said get out of there!"

"No, man! Not until I've nailed him *and* got a sixty-six-million-dollar fuck from the ranger bitch with him!"

"I said, get out of there now!" Qualen snapped off the radio. He looked at Kristel, who had walked back. "That may take a while. Catching Gabriel, I mean." He motioned for Delmar to join them.

"Do you believe him?" Kristel asked.

"About Mr. Walker? I'm afraid I do. He was outside all night, and that's not exactly an explanation one would just dream up. I imagine he took as much pleasure burning the money as *I* will burning his friend."

Kristel was trembling with anger. Delmar arrived, dragging Hal, his hand around the ranger's throat.

"Never mind," Qualen said. "There's still one third of the money to find, and two thirds of the ranger team to hunt down."

"Which do we do first?" Delmar asked.

"Kristel, bring the C-4. I don't want Mr. Walker making any more trouble for us."

"What about Kynette?" Kristel asked.

Qualen pushed Hal back in the direction they'd come. "He's applying for early retirement."

Delmar grinned. "Good. It'll save me the time of whacking him myself."

FIFTY-TWO

"We've got another problem," Gabe said.

He was slightly ahead of Jessie in the sloping passageway, listening to see when it might be safe to return.

"I think we've got more company."

He moved ahead and listened again. He heard the rustle of cloth, of pebbles and dirt hitting the ground. "He's coming. Where's the pick?"

She pointed ahead. "Where the passage heads straight up. Right where you left it."

"Great. All we've got are rusty pitons. We can give him tetanus."

"If you can get close enough."

Despite the jokes, Gabe was nervous. The bruises on his chest and back were sore, and he was looking at a knockdown drag-out with Clubber Lang's big brother.

"What are we going to do?" Jessie asked.

Gabe thought for a moment, then motioned her backwards. "Ready?" he whispered.

She nodded, and Gabe moved into position.

There was no light other than the distant daylight filtering in from above.

Gabe leaned back against the wall, breathing as quietly and as shallowly as he could.

Kynette dropped to the bottom of the vertical passage just a few feet away.

Gabe said, "If you want me, I'm here."

Kynette stopped in his tracks on the other side of the rock formation.

"You're making this too easy for me, Walker," Kynette said as he rounded the rock.

Kynette obviously didn't see him. The big man walked along, looking ahead.

Gabe saw the machine gun, which was in Kynette's right hand. He saw the bastard raise it.

"Over here!" Gabe shouted.

Kynette turned back, ready to fight. As he did, Jessie dropped from the roof and slammed her boot into his head.

Kynette hardly felt it. He raised a hammerlike fist and backhanded her; Jessie flew a few feet and hit the floor, stunned.

"You fuck!" Gabe raged, and threw himself at the big man.

Kynette's radio clattered into a gully as he fell back.

"Jess!" Gabe cried out, "get the—"

He didn't get to finish, as Kynette recovered and came after him, lifting Gabe with his knees and throwing him off. Gabe landed on his back, the wind knocked out of him, but he managed to scramble to his feet to meet Kynette's next charge.

The big man threw a succession of kung-fu kicks and punches at him, knocking Gabe back as they connected with his arms, sides, and legs.

Kynette was toying with him.

"What'samatter, tough guy?" Kynette laughed. "Didn't they teach you self-defense in ranger school?"

Gabe said nothing, just took the punishment as he watched Jessie rise behind Kynette. She reached for his gun, picked it up, and fired.

There was a weak, helpless *click*.

Kynette turned and grinned. "No bullets, bitch!" He laughed, then spun and kicked Gabe hard, sending him over a rock and onto his back.

Kynette drew a gold-handled Bowie knife from a sheath and, slowly walking to Gabe's side, grabbed a handful of his hair.

Jessie started toward him, but Kynette made a threatening gesture with the knife.

She stopped.

He turned to Gabe. "I'm going to ask you three times: where's the money? I want it."

"I—I can't help you," Gabe moaned.

Kynette kicked him in the side.

"Wrong answer. I'm going to ask you two times: where's the money?"

Gabe struggled up from the blow, collapsing as his feet slid from under him.

Kynette pulled him up by the hair and smiled.

"Where's the money?"

Gabe shook his head.

"I'm going to ask you one more time: where's the money?"

Gabe said nothing.

Kynette grinned. "Time to kill a mountain man," he said. "You know, it amazes me in this day and age that a man would put money before the personal safety of himself and his bitch. At least you can go to your grave knowing that I'm going to treat the bitch right."

Kynette held the knife before Gabe's eyes, showing it to him, taunting him. With his last ounce of energy, Gabe reached his right hand out and grabbed Kynette's crotch, put his left hand to the big man's chest, and lunged at him.

Tucking his shoulder into Kynette, Gabe shoved him back and up, toward a stalactite: blood and death cries poured from him as the rock plunged through his upper back.

Gabe stayed beneath him, growling, pushing, and pouring out his anger over Evan and Hal and everything else that had happened as Kynette clawed weakly at his head.

He stopped only when Kynette stopped moving. He stepped back, away from where the body hung grotesquely, dripping blood onto the tunnel floor. Gravity finally did its work and pulled the body down. It hit the ground with a wet smack.

Jessie staggered around it and hugged Gabe.

"I'm sorry I got you into all this."

"It's all right," he said.

Breaking the embrace, Gabe went to the body, felt for extra clips, and found his bolt gun on Kynette's equipment belt. He took it, just as a familiar voice crackled through the tunnel.

"Jessie, Hal, come in . . . please report. Over."

"It's Frank. Where's the radio?"

They looked at each other for a moment, then bolted toward the gully in the tunnel floor. Gabe shoved his arm back in, straining as the sharp edge cut against his underarm.

"Jessie," Frank went on, "I don't know if you can read this, but all hell is heating up. We found Evan. He's hurt, but he's alive. LifeStar is flying him to the hospital right now. Do you read? Over."

"Damn . . . damn . . . damn . . ." Gabe said, unable to respond to Frank.

"Hal," Frank said, patient as St. Francis, "Jessie, report in . . . please. Hal, Jess—!"

"Help me!"

Another voice came from the radio. It was Kristel's. "Oh, no," Jessie said.

"Please . . . help us!"

"I copy," Frank replied. "Where are you? Over!"

"I'm on a flat area near a pyramid-shaped rock formation . . . about a half-mile from a bridge behind the peak I'm on."

"Lyin' bitch!" Gabe said under his breath.

"I think I know where you are," Frank said. "Hang on. I'll be there in two shakes."

Above, Gabe heard Qualen say, "Someday, Kristel, you'll make somebody a great wife."

She said, "You should see me bake a cake."

Jessie frowned. "Gabe, you've *got* to get it! Frank has no idea—they'll kill him!"

He nodded in agreement, just as he heard something that made his day.

Worse.

FIFTY-THREE

Qualen and Kristel walked across the bridge, where Hal, Delmar, and Travers were waiting. Hal had heard Kristel's call on the other walkie-talkie, still in Delmar's hand, and knew what it meant.

They had called Frank to come and get them. They could take their time, get the money, steal the chopper, and fly off. It would be days before anyone came up here to investigate. Even a search party wouldn't think to come up this high.

"You'll be happy to know," Qualen said to Hal, "that your friends are still alive"—he looked at his watch—"at least, for another three minutes annnnd . . . one second."

"It's set?" Travers said. "We'll finally be rid of him?"

"All of them?" Delmar added.

"Primed to go off right over their heads."

FIFTY-FOUR

When he heard Frank's transmission, Gabe pulled his arm from the gully, snatched up the bolt gun, and pushed Jessie back toward the diagonal passageway.

"Take this," he said, throwing her Douglas's rope.

"Gabe—whatever you're planning won't work! This rope is sixty years old!"

"That's eight in dog years," Gabe said. "It's also all we've got."

He bent her down into the tunnel and followed her, both on their backsides, sliding, using their fast-moving feet as brakes. Gabe was keeping a rough count in his head. This was going to be close—and even if his plan worked, there was no guarantee that the blast wouldn't dump the mountaintop on their heads, burying the passageways and shafts from top to bottom. They reached the edge and burst out into the light with about ninety seconds to go, and heard the beat of the oncoming chopper's rotor.

"Frank!" Jessie said. "No, Frank . . . *Frank!*"

She waved wildly, but it was no use.

Gabe handed her the rope. "Here. Unravel this."

She fed him the first piece and knotted the others end-to-end as Gabe attached the rope to a carabiner. He bolted it to the floor of the ledge and threw the rope over the edge. It looked like ninety feet of twine.

"Gabe, this'll never hold."

"It'll have to. Now go!"

Jessie clearly wasn't convinced, but she started to rappel down. When she'd gone a few feet he began to rappel after her ... with, by his count, just over a minute to detonation.

Gabe got bad news right away. The rope didn't sag at all; it had no moisture, no give. Though Gabe had anticipated that, he hadn't expected it to fray as quickly as it did, every lateral move dragging it against the rock face and causing fibers to snap. He could feel them unwinding and falling on his hands.

The only safe place was a niche in the rock wall, some fifteen feet away.

"We'll have to swing you over!" Gabe said, his voice tense.

"Gabe, no! The rope won't take it!"

"Hold tight, we're doin' it!" he said. "Swing and drop."

They had about thirty seconds. He put his feet against the wall and they began to run against it, pushing off and then swinging out in a wide arc that brought them closer to the cave but not close enough. Bending his legs, he kicked out again, the two of them flying back, Jessie getting a larger swing this time. She leaned toward the wall, holding the rope with just one hand, and they kicked off a third time.

They swung out at a dizzying height, arcing toward the cave. Gabe caught his feet on the ledge, landing on it, but Jessie tumbled over the edge.

"Gabe!"

She still had one hand on the rope, her boots scraping the wall for a foothold as she tried to reach up with her free hand. If the explosives went off now, the blast would shake her free.

"Hold on, Jess! Hold on—and reach up!"

She tried, but couldn't reach him.

"I can't, Gabe!"

Gabe's hand flashed out, getting a tenuous grip on her forearm. She swung like a pendulum over the abyss; with each swing, her hand slipped further down his arm, his grip finally reaching wrist level.

Teeth clenched, eyes narrowed, he dug into Jessie's glove and held.

"Oh, God," she wailed. "Please, oh God!"

Gabe looked down and saw Sarah below him, not Jessie.

"Reach up!" he yelled. "*Do* it!"

"*Gabe!*" she gasped, struggling vainly to reach him.

"*Reach me!*" he cried.

As she struggled to do so, he gripped the ledge and pulled her toward it. Without thinking, he'd offered her the arm that he'd had down the fissure, and it was fading fast. His muscles were trembling, on empty, and with the last ounce of life that was left in them, Gabe hoisted her onto the lip and followed her into the rocky niche, throwing himself on top of her as the world around them came alive.

The ground heaved an instant before the sound of the explosion reached them. The floor of the ledge shook violently and they were showered with pebbles and dirt; Jessie screamed but Gabe barely heard her as, beside them, the passage they'd left echoed with the thunder of boulders and earth raining from above. Clouds of dust rolled around them, Jessie and Gabe coughing then scampering to the edge when the air became too thick with dirt to breathe.

Within moments, the rumbling of the earth had stopped and all they heard was the patter of small stones and the distant crash of rocks tumbling down the vertical passageway, cracking and dislodging stalactites and stalagmites which joined the muffled roar. And soon, even those sounds stopped.

Gabe and Jessie moved out from the safety of the small overhang. She leaned over and kissed Gabe's cheek.

"Thanks," she said. "I thought I was gone."

He looked up and around. "We'll have to go this way," he pointed up. "We're going to have to climb. You going to be all right?"

She nodded.

They followed the lip along the wall, one ledge leading to the next. They headed for what they hoped would be a way up; after nearly a half hour, they found it as they rounded a corner.

"I don't believe it," Gabe said, as he crawled over. "Something finally broke our way."

He pulled loose rocks from the edges. There was a thin ledge of rock a few feet below, and it led to a gentle slope spotted with boulders and tall grasses. The slope went down the Tower.

Gabe squirmed through the rift, then helped Jessie onto the ledge as they set off for the bridge.

He looked up, his palm held away, shielding his eyes from the bright sun.

"This is the northern ridge," Jessie said. "Gabe, we're on the wrong side of the Tower."

"I know. Crockett River is where the last of the money fell."

"Meaning if we follow this slope straight up, we can still get to the bridge and over."

"There's no 'we,'" Gabe said. "What you're doing is going back down to the station to get help."

"Forget it! I stayed with you this far, and I'm staying all the way."

"Look, there's no time to argue! As it is, we can only get there first if Hal busts their chops a little—"

"Right. So let's go." She started up the ridge toward the slope. "You coming?"

"God—you're the toughest man I know!" Gabe yelled, then trudged after her, looking past his pain, past the moment, thinking only about the money, the case on which all of their lives might well depend.

FIFTY-FIVE

The helicopter banked toward a dip on the mountaintop, its tail wheel touching the ground first, followed by its two main undercarriage wheels. The chopper settled down, its skids nearly touching the rise in the ground. Snow was swept into high-rising plumes and spirals by the churning rotors.

Hal was out of sight, lying facedown in the dirt. Travers had his arm locked behind him and Qualen had his knee against his back, a pistol rammed against the base of his neck. The ranger could see Kristel also lying facedown, several feet from the chopper. Frank would see her and think she was hurt or dead.

He was helpless. As helpless to prevent his friend from blundering into disaster as he was to prevent the death of Gabe. He saw Delmar squatting behind a boulder, a machine gun in his hands. He watched Frank leave the chopper, ducking as he ran forward.

"What the hell happened here?"

"I was hoping you could tell us!" Kristel said. "Welcome."

Frank was stunned as she sat up quickly and snatched

the gun from his holster. She aimed it at his face.

"What're you doing?" Frank asked. "I came here to help you all."

"You did." Delmar grinned and fired, bullets chewing up the snow all around.

The ranger flew backward, propelled by a spray of blood; he landed on his back.

Kristel leapt from the ground and screamed, "What the hell do you think you're doing, Delmar? Who told you to fire?"

Qualen rose and Hal jumped to his feet. He ran and dropped beside his friend.

"Frank . . . Frank . . ."

"We're moving out!" Qualen announced, wielding his shotgun like a saber and pointing to the chopper.

Hal gazed down on his friend, still barely alive and trying to get something across to him. No one saw him slip the folding knife from his belt and into Hal's hand; then Frank wheezed, and Hal saw the life run from him.

"This man never hurt anybody," Hal said gravely.

"Never said he did." Qualen leveled the gun menacingly at Hal. "His reputation is still unsullied." He looked over at Kristel. "Check the chopper and let's go."

Hal slipped the knife into his boot and covered Frank's face with a kerchief. He glared at Qualen, then turned to go. For now, there was nothing else to do.

FIFTY-SIX

Except for the cold wind knifing through the rips in Gabe's sweater, it was an easy walk up the slope. They passed the ledge, Lover's Ledge, without comment and continued up, where the slope became steeper. Still, they were able to walk it, and in three-quarters of an hour had made it to the last leg of the journey: a four-thousand-foot chasm spanned by a rope and timber bridge built by Gordon Douglas.

Gabe hesitated. He watched the twenty-yard span rock in the wind.

"Man, I hate these goddam things. I'd rather climb a sheer face. At least I'm in control of that."

He started across the bridge, Jessie waiting a few moments and then following, keeping their weight distributed several feet apart. As Gabe approached the other side, something shifted underfoot, in the sunlight. Something like a spider web.

Gabe felt the tug as he passed it, realized too late that it was a tripwire. He stopped and glanced up just long enough to see the timer attached to the stake that held up the bridge.

"Go back!" he yelled, running toward Jessie.

She paused, confused.

"They've wired it to blow!" he shouted.

Jessie ran and reached the end of the bridge. She turned just in time to see a ball of fire erupt from the other side. The bridge broke loose and snapped halfway across the chasm before the two halves fell.

Gabe was only a few feet from the cliff as the bridge dropped from under him. Legs coiling, he launched himself at the stakes, which were still firmly embedded in the rock. Jessie grabbed him by the backpack and, straining hard, helped him up. She hugged him to her.

"You son of a bitch!" Gabe yelled across the chasm. He rose as his voice echoed through the mountain and died.

"What now?" Jessie asked.

Gabe pushed a hand through his hair.

"I can still make it if I go along the north wall to Bitker's Ladder," he said. "This time we're not going to argue! Somebody's got to go after them, and somebody's got to go back and get reinforcements. I stand a better chance of getting to the ladder and beating these fucks there."

She nodded. "All right, Gabe. But be careful."

He waved and, reluctantly, she turned and headed back down the ledge.

FIFTY-SEVEN

At the helicopter, Qualen swapped Delmar shotgun for machine gun. Then he walked over to Kristel, who had been examining the instrument panel. She said something to him and he nodded, poked his head into the cabin. After a moment, he shut the ignition and pocketed the key.

"What the hell are you doing?" Travers asked.

Kristel said, "There's not enough fuel to search around. Just enough to get us down once we find the money."

"But we can't *walk* there—"

"Why not?" Qualen asked. "You couldn't ask for better weather."

"But they're sure to have found the Treasury jet by now—"

"Doubtless."

"And someone may have spotted your jet."

"Likely."

"So there's no time to dick around! Let's fly till we find the money, make sure we get it!"

"Oh, we'll get it," Qualen assured him. "We have a hostage, and we still have the chopper. We're really okay."

"Okay? We're hunted, low on fuel, and shy sixty-odd million bucks! Let's at least make sure this isn't a total washout!"

Qualen said, "Travers, you'd do well to remember two things. First: we wouldn't be here if you hadn't fucked up. Second: you're not running things. I am. If you're worried about getting out, you can start walking—now."

Travers glared at him.

"Is that a yea or nay?" Qualen asked.

Travers threw up his hands. "Do I have a choice?" Switching the monitor on, he glanced at it and started toward the money.

Hal walked up behind him, a few paces ahead of Delmar.

"Guess what, Travers. You and I have something in common."

"Piss off."

"Sure. Just as soon as you remember a third thing: when Qualen finds the money, you're as dead as me. Got that, agent? Qualen's nothing but a thug. It's gonna be you and me, back of the head, hit-style."

Travers walked to the other side of the chopper, glaring again at Qualen. He touched something on the monitor. Qualen saw what he did and regarded Hal.

Hal could see the criminal's mind working, running over ways this could all still go south for him. The ranger wasn't surprised when Qualen suddenly put up his hand and approached Travers.

Delmar and Kristel stopped.

"Give me the monitor," Qualen snapped. "Now."

Travers was strangely nonchalant as he slipped the unit from his neck and slid it across the chopper's bay.

Qualen looked down at it as the screen went black. His lips tight, eyes narrow, he said, "What's the code, Travers?"

"You're the boss, you figure it out. There's fifty thousand possible keycode combinations, in fifteen-second intervals."

Qualen's hands became fists. "Give me the fucking code, Travers."

Travers whipped out a pistol that was hidden in his back pocket. "I don't think so, *Mr.* Qualen. I'm a partner in this enterprise, and I intend to have some say in what goes down."

Qualen's brows rose. "So . . . a survivor! So what's the plan, agent? Use the chopper to find the money? Walk to town, steal a car, and just drive out?"

"That's better by a half than what *you* want to do."

"That's a matter of opinion, agent. In any case, we *will* do it my way." He stepped up behind Kristel and pulled her in front of him as a shield.

"Eric!" she rasped. "What're you doing?"

She looked over her shoulder at him. It was the first time Hal had ever seen fear in her eyes; he actually hurt for her.

Qualen stroked her cheek affectionately and spoke into her ear, "You know what real *love* is, Kristel?"

"No—"

He smiled. *"Sacrifice."*

Two short, muffled bursts rose from between them, and blood blossomed on the front of Kristel's jacket. There was shock and sadness on her face as Qualen released her; she dropped facedown onto the deck of the chopper. The pistol was still smoking.

Qualen looked at Travers, whose expression was a mix of terror and revulsion.

"Now, Agent Travers, I'm the only one who can fly us out of here." Qualen walked toward him slowly, and pulled the gun away. Then he angrily slid the monitor back to him. "Now, Agent Travers, go and get *our* money."

Qualen grabbed Kristel's coat, pulled her from the chopper, and let the body drop to the ground.

"I'll be waiting here until then," Qualen said, "just in case anyone spots the chopper and tries to ground us. Radio back when you find the money and I'll come and get you."

"Gotcha," Delmar said. "Good plan."

Qualen handed him Travers's automatic weapon. Delmar pointed it at Hal.

"And Delmar? If Mr. Tucker so much as looks in our partner's direction again, shoot him in the arm. The elbow. Not a lot of blood, but a great deal of pain."

Delmar gave him a little salute, then pushed Hal ahead. "Move it out, a-holes. I wanna be home in time for dinner."

Hal walked, though he was damned if he'd expedite things for them. There was a peak they could cross to get to the money faster; he was going to avoid it, lead them south, make it so they'd have to cross Crockett River to get where they were going. And if the police or FBI. showed up in the meantime, he'd blow his own brains out rather than let them take him hostage.

They'd killed Gabe and Frank. They were going down.

FIFTY-EIGHT

Gabe climbed to a ledge that was thirty feet up, then followed it along. The ledge was no more than sixteen inches across at its widest, and in most places it was nine or ten. It rose and sunk as it followed the peak to the top, and there were gaps up to a yard wide in spots. Only experienced climbers ever came this far, and only thrill-seekers went higher. Thrill-seekers . . . or someone with a purpose.

Gabe's carriage defined *purpose*: jaw set, eyes steady, posture strong and erect, dirt, cuts, and bruises the only evidence of the day's events. He jogged along the ledge, keeping up a steady pace, and even when his limbs began to complain, he was driven by a strange mix of contempt, hope, and determination. By the knowledge that Hal's life was in his hands, the same as Sarah's had been. By the need to stop Qualen—to prove to himself something he'd been doubting this past year: that right *can* make might.

The ledge ended at a ladder and a sign. The sign read, "Property of the Bitker Mining Company," and above it was a ladder, its metal rungs woven into loose steel cable bolted into the sheer rock face of the peak. The ladder started nine feet off the ground and continued another two hundred and forty-nine feet to the top of the peak.

Gabe stood under the ladder. The lowest rung was two feet above his outstretched hands.

"Bitker, you cheap bastard. Couldn't you afford two more feet?!"

No one had ever understood why it was built this way, but they knew this: if you jumped for the ladder and missed, it was a four-thousand-foot fall backward.

Gabe bent at the knees and sprung up, aiming to reach the second rung from the bottom; if he missed that, there was always one to fall back to. But he caught it and pulled himself up. After a breath-sapping climb up the ladder, he reached the top of the Tower—a flat, spectacular two-mile-by-two-mile region that had been described by some as God's Playground, by others as the Devil's Spa.

Gabe started forward. Before him was a kidney-shaped lake covered with ice that was thick near the shore and thin near the center, with smooth water poking through here and there. It was cut out in the middle of a solid rock formation, with the Crockett River winding away and down on the far side. A long, timber bridge had been built at an angle across one corner of the lake—something to make life easy for hikers who had made it this far.

Something else was here as well: the money.

Gabe rattled a fist in triumph as he spotted the case buried in deep snow above the lake. It had taken a rough landing on the rock and had broken in half.

He hurried over and smiled. Small animals—wild hares, it looked like from the pawprints—had nibbled the edges of some of the bundles and obviously hadn't liked what they tasted.

He opened his backpack and began stuffing the cash into it. As he finished up, he had an idea. Snapping twigs from a branch, he followed the rabbit tracks through a tangle of brush to their source.

FIFTY-NINE

Hal, Delmar and Travers came up the long, winding slope. Travers paused to bend over, resting stiff-armed on his knees while he caught his breath, while Delmar leaned against a tree.

"Almost there," Travers said, standing up straight again and looking at his monitor. It was amazing how greed could overcome exhaustion. "I've got it locked in. Just a few hundred yards."

This was it, then. One of the men would probably go with him, Hal thought. He figured Delmar would be the one keeping him company. Fine. If he could use Frank's knife on the big guy, and get his gun, Travers would be a piece of cake.

He pulled off his glove and bent as though he were going to scratch inside his boot.

Delmar strode over and spun him around by the wrist. "Hey, if we're there, then you're done with him."

Travers looked at Hal and nodded. "Yes, but for God's sake do it quietly. Your insane boss made enough noise back there for anyone within ten miles to hear us. We don't need to give them a second beacon."

Looking down at the monitor again, Travers moved away.

Delmar was holding his automatic weapon in one hand, Hal's wrist in the other, and smiling. "You heard the man. You ready to die quietlike, asshole?"

Hal looked up into the dull gray eyes. "Hey, let's get something straight. If I'm gonna die, I'm gonna die. But you're always gonna be the asshole. So just shoot, all right?"

The big man grinned. "This ain't a shootin' war, soldier."

Delmar reared back and slammed his head against Hal's forehead, catching him totally off-guard and throwing him to the ground. Before he could recover, Delmar kicked him in the ribs.

"How we feelin'? Upset stomach, eh?"

Delmar kicked him in the chest again, sending Hal skidding back on the snow. He tried to rise, got as far as his hands and knees.

"Like soccer, ranger man? Great sport!" He slung his automatic over his shoulder. "I was a bloody good striker. Here's an outside right."

Delmar ran forward and kicked Hal in the lower leg. There was a snap, and Hal rolled to his side, howling in agony.

"Did I hear something break?"

Hal's right shin was numb, but he was determined to get up.

"Outside left!" Delmar yelled, kicking Hal in the right knee. Hal flew back several feet, crashing heavily on his side near the edge of the cliff. "No break, but a clean hit."

"Fuck you!" Hal said through his teeth.

"Cursin'. That's a penalty kick for unsportsmanlike conduct!"

Delmar hit him once again, catching him in the front of the right thigh.

"A lovely chip shot to the winger!" Delmar cheered, holding both arms above his head and doing a little dance.

Hal reached down as though rubbing his shattered lower leg. His hand slipped into his boot.

"Winger back to striker!" Delmar said, running toward Hal and driving the toe of his boot into his broken shin. Hal screamed, and Delmar cheered again, ran in a circle in front of him. "He dribbles past the defender!" He kicked him in the gut. "Two defenders." Another kick. "Three defenders." Another.

Hal lay crumpled on his side, curled in a ball of pain.

Delmar jogged in place, facing him, staring at his head. "Striker lines up to the goal . . . focuses on the ball . . ."

Delmar backed up. He unzipped his coat. "The crowd is on its feet, the League Cup championship for this season comes down to this last kick. The striker sees an opening, draws back his foot—and fires!"

Delmar ran forward, kicking Hal over the side of the cliff. Hal scrabbled for a handhold and, clinging desperately to the side, hung there as Delmar came over and stepped on his fingers, pinning him to the cliff face.

As Delmar grinned down at him, Hal found the knife in his boot. Clandestinely opening the blade, he slammed it into Delmar's leg. With an agonizing scream, Delmar doubled forward as, with a desperate lunge, Hal reached up and grabbed the rifle hanging from its strap on Delmar's shoulder. He jammed it into his chest.

"You choked, big guy," Hal said. He leveled the gun at his chest. "And now, asshole—the season's over!"

He fired at close range, a blotch of red spraying across

Delmar's chest, a stream of blood spraying from his back. The Englishman flew into the air and over Hal's head, soaring down the cliff.

Hal climbed slowly off the cliff face, grasping a tree for support. Then, limping painfully to the riverbank, he picked up the automatic weapon and hobbled across the river to find Travers.

SIXTY

"I said quietly, shithead," Travers said to himself, not looking back as he studied the monitor.

Something strange was going on.

He had pinpointed the case just a minute before, two hundred yards due west. He looked up at the sun: he was headed due west, but the case was now three hundred yards away.

He rekeyed the code, just to make sure he'd done it correctly. The blip appeared on the grid.

"What the hell?"

The case was seventy-five yards to the southwest. And moving.

"It can't be!" He glared across the snow-swept terrain to the lake. "It *can't* be!"

Holding the monitor in front of him, like a divining rod, Travers ran in the direction of the blip, moving toward the lake, then to the west, then slogging up a hill to the southwest. All the while, the damn thing remained seventy-five to eighty yards away.

He stopped to catch his breath. The blip started moving toward him. He stared at the monitor, watched as the blip moved to within seventy yards, sixty, closer—

Someone had the case; that was the only explanation. He took out an automatic, held it in front of him, and waited.

Then he saw it. The blinking red light. Draped like a necklace around a large, brown winter rabbit.

Travers screamed and the rabbit fled. The agent shot at it anyway, tearing up trees and snow, then fumbled for his radio.

"Come in!" he shouted. "*Come in!*"

Clear and calm, Qualen said, "From your excitement, I take it you've got what we need?"

"No, I don't! That son of a bitch Walker is alive, Qualen!"

"No names, this is an open line!"

"Ask me if I *give* a shit, Eric Qualen! I had to be insane ever to tie up with a lowlife piece of shit like you. He beat us. A fuckin' hick mountain ranger beat the man no law agency ever could! If I weren't so fuckin' blown away, I'd want to shake that bastard's hand!"

"Get off the radio!" Qualen's voice was no longer calm.

"Why? I've got something to be afraid of? I've got *nothing*, man!"

"I said stop transmitting, you stupid bastard!"

Travers flopped down in the snow. He shook his head. "It's hard to believe I sold out after twenty years and this is the payback—to rot on a mountain with a fucking dirtbag like you."

"You're losing it, Travers—it's not over."

"Losing it? You finally got it right, Qualen. I'm pure Section Eight. But you're right. It's not over. I've gotta go. I'm late for my last official manhunt."

Travers rose, turned off the radio, and dusted the snow from his pants.

"You may be smart, Walker, but you can't fly. And if you can't fly, there are gonna be footprints."

Tossing the monitor aside, his gun at his side, eyes on the ground, Qualen, Delmar, and Hal forgotten, Travers launched his own private war.

SIXTY-ONE

"Jesus Christ!" Wright yelled as he listened to the single headphone pressed to his ear. "Did you hear that, Davis?"

"Yes, sir."

"That's Travers. They're alive." Wright leaned forward and tapped the pilot on the shoulder. "Did you get a bead on that frequency?"

She nodded. "Judging from the strength of the signal and the direction, they're about ten miles to the north, in the open, about a mile up. I can get us pretty close, and we can eyeball it from there."

"Good," Wright said. "Let the FBI guys know that the two miserable bastards are down there somewhere, and not to move in until we know exactly where. I don't want them coming in like *Apocalypse Now* and scaring them into hiding."

LaFond said, "I'll tell them—but the FBI has its own way of doing things!"

"I know," he said. "That's why I don't want you to tell them *where* we are until we've got visuals on the two." Wright sat back. "I don't want this Qualen making off with

191

our money . . . but I *really* don't want Travers to get away. And ask if they can find out who this Ranger Walker is. I may want to kiss the guy."

He squeezed the handrests again as LaFond simultaneously nosed down and swung to the north. But he couldn't wipe the smile from his face: as he'd always suspected, there *was* a God, and He was squarely on the side of the Treasury Department.

SIXTY-TWO

Weighted down by his bundle full of frozen assets, Gabe wasn't making the kind of time he'd hoped to make. But he pressed on, wanting to get back to Bitker's Ladder and down the ledge, in among the peaks and fissures, where he wasn't as exposed as he was here.

He was on the long eastern slope leading to the lake when bullets chewed up the ground behind him.

He jumped ahead, ducked beside a tree, and looked back.

It was Travers. He was striding toward him, shoulders stiff, head bent forward, the automatic tucked against his side and pointed ahead. He looked like a robot killer from a science fiction film, his little laser eyes searching for prey.

Travers spit a second burst of gunfire at the tree. It tore up the branches above Gabe's head, and they rained down in splinters. He looked around quickly. He not only had to put some distance between them, but on rough terrain as well. He'd do better on that than Travers would.

Pushing off against the tree, Gabe ran toward the only shortcut he knew.

A short burst grazed his side.

Breaking into a run, he hurried toward the nearly vertical bank that sloped down to the lake. As he did, there was another burst of fire, followed by a thud as a bullet lodged in a nearby tree.

Gabe leapt ahead, praying that the trees would break his fall. One did, but his momentum carried him hard into another tree, which spun him around and over a ledge. He landed hard at the edge of the lake.

He struggled to his feet, reached around to his side. The wound wasn't bad, though it was bleeding. He looked around. This wasn't where he wanted to be: Travers would have a clear shot at him.

There was only one thing to do, and Gabe started doing it, climbing painfully up onto the bridge.

SIXTY-THREE

Jessie was hiking at a slow but steady pace down the gentle slopes on the east side of the Tower, tired and sore and alternately cursing Gabe and wishing he were there.

She wanted him to come back to her. More than anything, she wanted to love him and grow old with him.

She stopped as she heard a familiar sound in the distance.

She listened; it was coming from below.

The chopper.

"Frank!" she cried, her face brightening. "You're beautiful!"

She ran toward the edge of the Tower, wondering how Hal had managed to warn him off, reaching the cliff just as the Huey Ranger rose from the expansive valley beyond.

The red drained from her cheeks as her eyes locked on those of the man at the controls. He had his arm pointed out the window, an automatic weapon trained on her.

It wasn't Frank. It was Qualen.

SIXTY-FOUR

Gabe wished he could stop bleeding. If anything was going to blow this, the steady drip of blood into a pool on the ice below him was it.

He'd climbed to the timbers underneath the bridge and wedged himself into an X-shaped configuration under the span. He'd tucked the money there as well: he would need freedom of movement to do what he had to do.

Travers had reached the bridge and stopped. Bent. Saw the blood. And followed it onto the bridge.

This wasn't going to be a free ride; Gabe knew he'd have to fight to get out of this. And he'd have to take the initiative, since Travers would be leading with a slug.

He also knew this was going to hurt them both: it was a long fall.

Gabe heard the timbers creak as Travers walked cautiously along the worn and rotted boards.

He had obviously seen the drops of blood leading toward the opening between the rocks at the end of the bridge.

A step at a time, listening for any telltale noise, Travers moved slowly along the bridge.

Suddenly, two hands shot through a gap in the bridge planks and yanked Travers through the boards by his ankles. But the same move had cost Gabe his balance and he crashed down, releasing Travers, falling through the ice.

Travers landed on the ice, and though his gun skidded away, the ice held.

It took an instant for the cold to seep through his clothing, but when it did Gabe felt as if he wanted to die . . . and would probably get his wish.

His eyes were open and the water was pure and clear. Save for his heart, thudding heavily in his ears, the silence was absolute. The current carried him slowly from the hole, and the diffused, hazy rays of the sun made it impossible for him to pick it out again.

Still facing up, trying to keep a grip on the situation, he paddled to bring himself back toward the surface. It was more difficult than he expected; something was weighting him down. He stripped off the water-logged sweater and T-shirt in a desperate attempt to keep from sinking. That done, he felt all around, searching for the hole.

It was nowhere. His lungs bursting, he tried floating on his back while he punched up with his fist and then his feet, trying to break a hole in the ice.

It refused to give.

He looked up through the cloudy ice and saw a shadow walking slowly toward him. Gabe reached into his equipment belt. Tingling from the bitter bite of the water, his fingers closed around his bolt gun. He slipped it out and waited.

The air was running out. His body was going numb.

He could feel his heart fighting to keep blood in his extremities.

Travers stopped right above him. A long shadow moved at his side—the automatic. Obviously, he'd found the money. Or he didn't give a shit where it was and wanted Gabe.

Gabe pushed the mouth of the bolt gun up against the ice. He fired.

The ice bulged up under Travers. The agent threw his arms up and Gabe thrust his head through the break in the ice. Between gasps, Gabe could see that the long bolt had buried itself in Travers's chest. The agent's mouth was wide with shock, eyes big and staring, and he fell dead, plunging through the hole Gabe had made when he fell from the bridge.

Gabe dropped the bolt gun. He hadn't had a chance to draw breath, and he had to fight to keep his lungs from pulling down water. His mind was spinning, eyes throbbing, ears prickling, everything on the verge of shutting down. Travers's body was beside him, settling and floating peacefully away, ribbons of red streaming from his chest where the bolt had struck.

Gabe's eyes closed and his mouth opened as his lungs were about to win the battle to take *something* in; suddenly, he felt himself being pulled upward, toward the light, toward the warm sun, toward life—

It was air, not water, that he pulled into his lungs. Gabe just lay on the ice, drinking air down in big gulps.

A familiar voice said, "You may know your way around a mountain, but you never could swim worth a damn."

Gabe opened his eyes. And smiled up at Hal.

". . . I'll take lessons."

Hal removed his jacket and placed it over Gabe's torso. Then he started frantically rubbing his legs and arms. Hal knew what he was doing, and Gabe warmed quickly, his limbs tingling as the blood returned to them.

"Don't get the wrong idea, Gabe. You're not my type."

"Too bad," Gabe said. "I could go for a husky ranger like you."

Hal grinned. "I think you're already spoken for. Where'd you leave Jessie?"

"Near Freedom Falls. She went for help." Gabe got up on an elbow. "What about the rest of the gang?"

"Qualen's the only one left. I took out Delmar. Qualen took out Kristel." His voice grew bitter. "They also got Frank, Gabe."

Gabe felt as if he'd been punched in the chest.

"Two years from retirement, all the guy wanted to do was fuckin' paint," Hal said.

Hal helped Gabe sit up, then reached into the hole in the ice. He cupped water into his hand and splashed it on the wound in Gabe's side.

"Not bad. Slugs cut clean through the flesh. You'll live."

He took a handkerchief from his pocket. His expression grew serious as he began wrapping it around Gabe's side. "Hey, Gabe . . . about Sarah. I know you did what you could."

Gabe looked down at his lap. "I tried."

"All these months, you were the guy I needed to talk to most—but if I did, I'd've had to start blaming the guy who was really responsible, the guy who'd brought her—"

A radio crackled to life.

"Travers, come in!"

Hal pulled the radio from his pocket. "Compliments of

Delmar," he said and punched the radio on. "It's too late, Qualen. You missed him. He decided to swim to Arizona—underwater."

There was a short pause. "Tucker?"

"That's right."

"Why am I not surprised?"

" 'Cause you're not quite as dumb as the rest of your late team."

Hal offered Gabe the radio and he took it from his friend.

"It's all over, Qualen."

There was a long pause. "Walker? You're alive too?"

"Yup."

"Good. You have the last of the money?"

Gabe shook his head. "Man, you don't know when to give up."

"On the contrary. I give up when I'm beaten. But I'm not, you see. I want that money and I want it now."

"Qualen, the game's over—you lost."

"No, the game's not over. I'm airborne now, you see, and as a matter of fact I picked up a passenger you might be interested in."

Gabe's expression sobered quickly.

"Go on, talk," Qualen was urging someone. "I said *talk*, goddammit!"

"Gabe . . . Hal—he's got me."

Gabe's bowels constricted. He shut his eyes and rolled his head.

"I'm sorry. I thought it was Frank, and—"

"Enough airtime, sweetheart," Qualen cut in. "So, have you got the picture, Walker? "Our business is not quite concluded: I want the money. Meet me at the highest point from where you are. Don't show up, and we're going to see if your angel here can fly."

"Jessie," Gabe said, "take him to the top of Bitker's Ladder. I'll meet you there."

Qualen snickered. "Love's a killer, isn't it?"

SIXTY-FIVE

While Hal made himself a splint using branches, Gabe climbed up under the bridge. When he'd reclaimed the sack full of money, he shimmied back down to help his friend.

Hal stood, tested the splint. "And the bastard made fun of my boy scout training."

"Then you're gonna be okay?"

"Yeah, sure. But what do you mean? I'm going with you."

"Not on that leg."

"I can make it."

"I know," Gabe said as he threw the bundle over his good shoulder. "But I can make it faster. Besides, you'll be there in spirit, where it counts."

"Then at least take this," he said, holding out Delmar's automatic.

"You keep it. If Qualen sees it, it might ruin everything. Get up there as fast as you can. Something happens to me and you get a chance—waste him."

Gabe made sure the radio was secure in his equipment belt, then started toward the embankment.

The hike to Bitker's Ladder took just twenty minutes. Even as he neared the cliff above it, Gabe heard the roar of the chopper, looked back, and saw it swoop in low, duck and weave through the trees, then swing in over the lake. Gabe couldn't decide whether he was like a kid with a toy or desperate or crazy or all three. He had to be careful how he played this, or Jessie was dead.

He got into position, then waited as the chopper drew near.

The radio clicked on. "Where are you, Walker?"

Gabe slipped it from his belt. "You're getting warmer, Qualen."

The rotors whipped flakes of ice from the lake as the chopper buzzed across, the skids just feet from the surface at times. When it reached the shore, it swung right. Qualen stopped the whirlybird so suddenly it reminded Gabe of a rearing horse.

Not that he was surprised. He was standing on a spur seven thousand feet up and out over the valley below. He was holding the bag of money at arm's length, over the spur; all that was holding it together was Gabe's grip.

Gabe put the radio to his mouth. "I've got your luggage. Give me Jessie."

Slowly, Qualen pushed the chopper forward, circling Gabe like a cat, the whirlwind testing his footing. After two passes, he was back in front of Gabe, hovering ten yards away and above the valley. Through the window, Gabe could see Qualen holding a gun. In the near compartment Jessie's arms were raised, handcuffed to the overhead bulwark.

"How do I know you have it in there?" Qualen asked.

"Want me to let go so you can see?"

"Touché," Qualen said. "You know, I'm a little disappointed. I felt sure Mr. Tucker would be hanging around

203

somewhere, to see you die. He said he hates you, you know."

"Let's get this over with."

"Okay. Bring it over here or I'll kill her."

"You do, and the spring thaw is going to be worth a lot of cash."

"The money!" Qualen snarled.

"When she's safe!"

Gabe didn't move, even though this was a game of chicken he wasn't sure he could win. He wasn't dealing with a rational man; if Qualen's insanity got the upper hand, even an upper finger, he might just forget about the money, kill them both, and fly off to fight another day. But that was a chance Gabe had to take. Once Qualen had the money, they were dead.

The wind howled. Everything else, everyone else, was dead still.

Gabe's eyes were on Qualen. After seconds that seemed like hours, the criminal laid the gun on the instrument panel and handed Jessie the keys to the cuffs. Gabe breathed again.

The helicopter crept forward, and Jessie went to the door. Qualen turned it so the door was facing Gabe; Jessie lowered herself down with the grappling cable. When Jessie reached the snowy surface, she started toward Gabe.

"Stay away!" he shouted. "Run!"

She hesitated. "What about you?"

"I'll do better with just me to worry about! Now *run*, dammit!"

Jessie stopped, thought for a moment, then ran in the opposite direction. She stopped behind a row of boulders.

Qualen was nearly over Gabe's head; his gun was trained on him through the open door.

"Now, Mr. Walker—throw the bag in."

Gabe looked up at Qualen.

"Let me have it!" Qualen screamed.

His arm stiff at his side, Gabe brought it back and threw the money, not at the door but well above it. It hit the rotor and disintegrated, paper locusts swirling around the helicopter, momentarily blinding Qualen.

Gabe used the distraction to duck under the chopper and grab the thirty-foot cable. While Qualen fired blindly, Gabe threw the hook over the top rung of Bitker's Ladder, then jumped back under the chopper as Qualen swept it around. Gabe crouched under the Ranger, moving with it as it edged back, dropping flat as Qualen suddenly changed direction and the tail rotor swung toward his head. Gabe knew he had to get out of there: sooner or later, one of Qualen's wild bursts would tag him. Either that, or the bastard would set the chopper down on his head.

Jumping to his feet, Gabe bolted toward the spur, grabbed the top rung of the ladder, and threw himself over the side just a step ahead of Qualen's speeding chopper.

As Gabe descended, the chopper nosed down and roared toward him, swinging out and around so Qualen could draw a bead on his foe. When it did so, the cable pulled taut, jolting the chopper and popping the bolts that held the top of the ladder in place. One of them blasted through the thin engine cowl over the cockpit; the turbine sparked and began to sputter, and as Qualen struggled to control the sinking helicopter, the ladder continued to rip away, Gabe clinging to the center.

SIXTY-SIX

"Gabe!"

Watching from four hundred yards away, Jessie ran from behind the rocks when the engine began to cough. As she emerged, a hand shot out and gripped her arm.

"Jessie, don't!"

She turned and saw Hal; he was looking past her, up at the chopper.

Taking aim with Travers's gun, he expended the remainder of the shells at Qualen and the chopper. When that failed to bring it down, Jessie tried to pull away. "Hal, let me *go*! We've got to try to—"

"Try to *what*? You can't reach him!"

"What are you *talking* about? We've got to *try*!" She looked toward the cliff and continued to struggle as the helicopter wobbled from side to side.

"Jess, don't! All Gabe's got right now is the knowledge that at least you're safe. Don't take that away from him!"

"But he's just *hanging* there—"

"And you can't help him!"

She stopped fighting. Hal was right. Gabe didn't need a cheerleader right now. What he needed was a rope—and she didn't have one.

She stared ahead, tears in her eyes. "Hal, I don't want to lose him."

"I know," he said softly, putting his arm around her. "Neither do I."

As they looked on, the powerful engine suddenly screeched and died; even before the shrill death rattle had faded, the rotor was grinding to a halt and the chopper had begun to fall.

SIXTY-SEVEN

Gabe's arms and legs were wrapped around the ladder when the chopper went down. The top of the ladder was twisted away from the ledge, bent almost back on itself, and there was no way of getting back to the top; the cable hook was out of reach and held in place by the weight of the descending bird, and there was nothing to do but hang on tightly as he watched the chopper fall.

Its tail rotor still spinning, the crippled whirlybird nosed down, tugging the winch cable taut; fluttering like a falling kite, it arced toward the cliff and smashed into the rock wall upside-down, side-first. The bolts in the lower half of the ladder held, though the top half wrenched down with a jolt, turning Gabe upside-down and shaking him free. He fell ten feet to the dangling chopper, landing on the skid.

Dazed, he got to his hands and knees, only to be thrown forward as a ladder bolt snapped and the chopper lurched violently. Gabe looked up as the ladder sagged to the right and the chopper tilted, sliding him toward the abyss. He grabbed hold of the skid and quickly glanced over his shoulder, scanning the cliff for a place to get off.

As he was eyeing a small ledge to the left—all he had to do was somehow get to it—he heard movement to the right. Looking over, he saw Qualen stick his head from the cockpit.

Grabbing hold of one another, the two men wrestled for position. Qualen climbed over the skid onto the upturned belly of the chopper, trying to kick Gabe's hands loose from the skid.

Gabe managed to grab one of Qualen's ankles and tip him onto his back. When Qualen went down, Gabe clambered up the chopper. As he climbed the skid, Qualen charged him again, trying to knock him into the valley; Gabe met his attack by ducking his shoulder and throwing him back into the mountainside.

The entire helicopter shook as he hit, the ladder groaning again, the whirlybird listing further toward the valley.

Gabe fell to his side, groaning as the wound there tore open.

"So Superman bleeds!" Qualen yelled triumphantly.

Gabe braced his foot against the skid and pushed off suddenly, rising and hitting Qualen. The two men landed hard on the chopper, Qualen spinning the weakened Gabe around, bending him back and trying to push his thumbs into his eyes. Gabe felt his wounded arm weakening and, in a desperate maneuver, ducked away from the cliff, using the slant of the chopper to get out from under Qualen. Then, grabbing the support strut to break his fall, he swung around and drove a hard right into the back of Qualen's neck.

Qualen fell face-forward and Gabe was on him in an instant, grabbing his hair, slamming his face into the metal, then flipping him onto his back and punching him repeatedly in the face.

The rung holding the cable hook sagged. The chopper listed again, and both men skidded. Qualen was slightly higher and fell onto Gabe, the two of them crashing against the skid. Qualen thrust his hand under Gabe's chin and choked him. Gabe tried in vain to pull his fingers loose.

The rung sagged again.

Qualen laughed louder. *"Looks like we go together, Walker!"*

Qualen had his weight down on his hand, and Gabe gave up trying to pull it away. Instead, he put everything he had into a blow to the side of his attacker's head. Qualen's grip weakened; Gabe slid out from under him and unleashed a flurry of overhand blows to the side of his head. Qualen fell to his side. Gabe turned and reached for the ladder, but Qualen had recovered and grabbed him around the legs. He pulled him down.

"Together, Walker!" Qualen cackled. *"You lost!"*

Gabe suddenly reared back, smashing the back of his skull into Qualen's face. He managed to grab Qualen by the neck with a stiff right arm and started to push him toward the edge of the chopper.

Dying was one thing. Gabe had faced it often enough, and that really didn't faze him. But he refused to give Qualen the satisfaction of taking him with him. Focusing himself as he had countless times before, on countless dangerous climbs and leaps and falls, he tensed his biceps and put everything he had into pushing Qualen over the edge.

Qualen's face and eyes were covered with blood; he was dazed from the blow he'd taken.

Gabe found added strength and, with one mighty heave, he threw Qualen to his knees.

With a look of surprise, Qualen twisted to try and grab his opponent. Gabe kicked him in the ribs. Qualen doubled over.

"I've got something to say to you!" Gabe cried.

He kicked Qualen again, dropping him to his hands and knees.

"You know what it is?"

He kicked him a third time, and Qualen fell to his side, sliding under the skid and into the cockpit.

"It's *fetch*, you fuck!" Gabe cried, then turned and scrambled toward the cable. He reached it just as the rung snapped in the middle; as the helicopter fell from underneath him, he jumped for the ladder, aiming for the second rung from the bottom, missing it, but catching the lowest rung. Gabe pulled himself up, hooking his arm around it, and looked back; Qualen was screaming, his mouth wide, as the chopper fell away. Gabe watched as it fell four thousand feet and erupted in a fireball when it hit the valley floor.

Gabe looked up. There were handholds aplenty to make up for the wrecked ladder, but his arms ached just thinking about another climb.

Just then, a chopper swung into view, full of agents. The man in the front seat was pointing, and Gabe looked up—just as the loop of a rope fell to within inches of his face. Beyond it, he saw the smiling faces of Jessie and Hal.

SIXTY-EIGHT

"It's Delmar's," Hal shouted down. "He's all finished with it."

Slowly, with painful effort, Gabe slipped the rope under one arm and then the other. Jessie pulled it tight.

"Remember," Hal said, "keep your arms and legs in the vehicle at all times."

Gabe smiled as he concentrated on the climb, using what little strength he could muster and letting Hal do the rest. When he reached the top, Jessie threw her arms around him, Gabe trying not to wince as she dug her chin into his wounded shoulder.

Hal dropped his end of the rope.

"Brother," he said, breathing heavily, "you think you could have put a little *less* effort into that climb? I thought you were in shape."

Gabe smiled. "Guess I'm just falling apart."

"I don't mind," Jessie said. "I'm great with repair work."

She put her hands around the back of his head and pulled his face to hers, kissing him as Hal's radio crackled to life.

"This is Walter Wright, Treasury Department. Over."

Hal stepped to the edge of the cliff and looked at the group in the chopper. "Copy. Over."

"Until the rescue team and local authorities arrive, everyone will remain where they are. Over."

Hal glanced back at his friends: they were pressed together from lips to thighs.

"Copy," he said, then turned, his eyes drifting down to the burning wreckage. "No one's going anywhere for a long time. Out."

SIGNET

Published or forthcoming

Against the Wind

J. F. Freedman

**'Bikers, murder, a bloodcurdling prison riot, and a powder-keg murder trial . . . It kept me up late into the night'
– Stephen King**

When Lone Wolf and his compatriots rode out of Santa Fe they left a trail of empty bottles, an alleged rape victim – and found themselves accused of a brutal murder.

Will Alexander was the hottest defence lawyer in New Mexico, in court and between the sheets. But life in the fast lane, a broken marriage and a serious drink problem had put his career on the skids.

The Scorpions lived their outlaw creed to the hilt. Will was convinced of their innocence, but soon he was fighting the case of his life. How could he defend men who held the law in open contempt?

'Delivers the kind of teasing ambivalence that makes for superior suspense' – *The New York Times Book Review*

SIGNET

Published or forthcoming

THE FEATHER MEN

Ranulph Fiennes

In the years between 1977 and 1990, a group of hired assassins known as the Clinic tracked down and killed four British soldiers, one at a time. Two of the victims were ex-SAS. All four had fought in the Arabian desert.

The Feather Men were recruited to hunt the Clinic. Without their intervention more soldiers would have died. At the end of their operation they asked Ranulph Fiennes, one of the world's best-known explorers and himself a former SAS officer, to tell their extraordinary story . . .

THE FEATHER MEN is the first account of a secret group with SAS connections – still unacknowledged by the Establishment – who set out to achieve their own form of justice. And how, in September 1990, they finally got their result . . .

SIGNET

Published or forthcoming

Riptide

Sam Llewellyn

Mick Savage was a fearless yachtsman and a renowned boatbuilder. Delivering a newly commissioned yacht to an old friend in France should have been a pleasure. So why was someone trying to kill him?

Fatally sabotaged, the *Arc-en-Ciel* should have sunk without trace in the black waters of the Bay of Biscay. Instead, Savage brought the tattered shell into La Rochelle and started looking for answers.

Beginning with the man he'd sailed with for half his life. The man who'd now disappeared – leaving behind a trail of fraud, extortion and violence that led from the stinking gutters of the South of France to the boardrooms of power in the City of London . . .

SIGNET

Published or forthcoming

THE FINAL TERROR

James Adams

Sana'a, North Yemen. Breakaway terrorist Abu Hassan unveils his ruthless plan to unite the leaders of the Palestine movement. A final, devastating act of terrorism ... *with the Palestinian state as the prize.*

This time there will be no single outrage. No targeted attack. Instead, a breathtaking all-out assault on the consumer markets of the West, resulting in hysteria no government will be powerful enough to control – or ignore ...

'James Adams, one of the world's best defence journalists, makes a stellar début with a first-class thriller' – Tom Clancy

'If there is a natural successor to Frederick Forsyth, it must be James Adams' – *Sunday Telegraph*

SIGNET

Published or forthcoming

Death Roll

Sam Llewellyn

The Tasman Sea, Australia. Martin Devereux sails in the trials for the America's Cup. It should be the high point of his yachting career. But a crash with arch rival Paul Welsh, a broken arm and a dead crew member send his challenge spiralling downwards.

Retreating to his boatyard on the English south coast, Devereux looks forward to life in the slow lane. But a series of suspicious accidents convinces him that the corruption is not ending but beginning.

Devereux finds connections that lead everywhere; to a girl with deep eyes and a deeper past, to Paul Welsh and his sinister cohorts. And to Spain, where the sunny waters are full of sharks. Human ones . . .

'An immaculately timed, tense adventure'
– *Mail on Sunday*

SIGNET

Published or forthcoming

THE SAS AT WAR
1941–1945

Anthony Kemp

The SAS are the most feared and respected elite fighting force in the modern military world. But what about the 'Originals', the valiant soldiers who turned an outlaw unit into one of the most effective strike forces of the Second World War?

First activated in 1941, Lieutenant David Stirling's 'L' detachment, Special Air Service, were the forerunners of today's SAS – taking part in more than 100 daring secret operations before being temporarily disbanded in 1945.

Until now, their story has never been definitively told.

Compiled with the help of previously unpublished military records and the accounts of the surviving Originals, THE SAS AT WAR reveals the truth about the early days of the Special Air Service, and shows how this unique fighting force overcame the disapproval of the military authorities to win glory and fame in North Africa, Italy and north-west Europe.